*

everything

NAN A. TALESE | DOUBLEDAY * *New York London Toronto Sydney Auckland*

*

everything A NOVEL

Kevin Canty

Copyright © 2010 by Kevin Canty

All rights reserved. Published in the United States by Nan A. Talese / Doubleday, a division of Random House, Inc., New York, and in Canada by Random House of Canada Limited, Toronto.

www.nanatalese.com

Doubleday is a registered trademark of Random House, Inc. Nan A. Talese and the colophon are trademarks of Random House, Inc.

LIBRARY OF CONGRESS CATALOGING-IN-PUBLICATION DATA
Canty, Kevin.
  Everything : a novel / Kevin Canty.—1st American ed.
    p.   cm.
  (alk. paper)
  1. Life change events—Fiction. 2. Montana—Fiction.
  I. Title.
  PS3553.A56E94 2010
  813'.54—dc22
  2009048197

ISBN 978-0-385-53330-0

PRINTED IN THE UNITED STATES OF AMERICA

10 9 8 7 6 5 4 3 2 1

First Edition

for Buck Crain

*

everything

*

The fifth of July, they went down to the river, RL and June, sat on the rocks with a bottle of Johnnie Walker Red and talked about Taylor. The fifth of July was Taylor's birthday and they did this every year. He would have been fifty. RL had been his boyhood friend and June was married to him. He'd been dead eleven years.

This side channel used to be one of Taylor's favorite fishing spots, but five or six years before, a beer distributor from Sacramento had built a twenty-room log home right on the bank and then drove a Cat D6 into the river and piled up a wing dam, to keep his house from falling into the drink. This pushed all the current out of the side channel and into the main river. A few last big fish lurked down deep in the channel but mainly it was suckers. Still, it was a pretty spot to sit on a long evening, the shade of the tall cottonwoods slowly deepening into green water. A pretty spot if you turned away from the log palazzo. They sat on the rocks and watched the water trickle by, the cool splash of river water over gravel.

I wish . . . said June.

You wish for what? RL asked her.

I wish I had a cigarette, she said, and laughed. June smoked exactly one day a year, and this was the day. RL got one out, gave it to her, lit it. He was smoking a cigar himself. He had bought the pack specially for her. The two of them stared at the smoke as it curled through the still air. RL could just barely hear the trucks passing on the interstate, a mile away. The sound always made him lonely, the thought of all that highway, all that American night out there.

These anniversaries, said June. They keep sneaking up on me. He's been gone, now, longer than I ever knew him.

That's not right.

No, I did the math last night. He was twenty-eight when I met him. twenty-eight to thirty-nine, thirty-nine to fifty. It doesn't seem like that long but it is.

Long time gone, said RL. I still, sometimes—I feel like I'm going to walk around a corner and see him on the sidewalk. You know, just sitting around the house, and I think, maybe I'll give Taylor a call, see if he wants to go grab a beer. Down at the Mo Club. See if I can borrow his pickup.

* * *

It's not like that for me, said June. Not anymore.

She reached for the square bottle of whiskey and took a demure pull on it. RL admired the workings of her throat, the little hollow at the base of her neck, her fine collarbone. She was younger than Taylor and him and still quite a good-looking girl.

I've been going to church again lately, she said.

Get the hell out of here.

I'm not kidding. Sunday morning ten o'clock.

Which one?

June blushed lightly. She was one of those transparent blondes where every feeling showed on her skin, pale or passionate. In tears she turned a blotchy red. RL had seen her in tears, not often.

I'm going to the Catholic one, said June. Weird, I know. A couple of the girls from work got me going there.

They got you all signed up? Human sacrifice in the basement and everything?

I think they quit doing that.

That's not what I hear.

It's safe to say that you would hate it, June said. I mean, you would hate even the good parts, which are all about doing good things and being nice to people in Central America and so on. They're so fucking earnest! But, you know, that's what I like about them.

You've always had an earnest streak.

And you've always been a cynical bastard.

With a heart as big as the great outdoors, RL said. That's me.

No, June said. That's somebody else.

Ten o'clock at night and the sun was well down, but the sky was lit a deep dark beautiful blue with the first few stars piercing it. The air was warm when it was still and then the river would blow a cool breeze through, rustling the leaves of the cottonwoods, riffling the water. RL felt a sadness in his chest that was like music, sad music. Taylor was gone, always gone. He had lived with this sadness eleven years until the jagged edges had worn smooth, like a river rock that he held in his hand, still warm from the day. RL felt almost a pleasure in it, the pleasure of touching something indisputable and real. He remembered the feeling of sitting in the waiting room at the hospital and holding her hand and waiting, that jagged feeling torn from him. Time had changed it into something different. *It's just like ice around my heart*, he thought, a line from a song he remembered. That wasn't it, exactly.

June said, I'll be standing in there singing a folk song and holding hands with some little old lady on either side of me and I'll just think, When did I turn into this? Peaceniks and bird-watchers.

Comfortable shoes, I bet.

* * *

Really comfortable shoes, said June.

Just then the bushes parted on the far side of the side channel, the island between them and the main branch of the river, and out into the twilight stepped a tall and serious-looking dark-headed girl with a baseball cap and a fishing pole. It was RL's daughter Layla, nineteen years old. In her shorts and sandals, in her long tan legs she waded the channel, water that swirled up to the hem of her shorts. She moved through the water almost silently, a fisherman's habit. *Trout are very nervous fish*, he remembered; a line from a book. She wore a Montana Grizzlies T-shirt and a kind of necklace from which dangled her forceps, her nippers and Gink.

Do any good? RL called out.

Layla came the rest of the way across the channel before she answered. Her power over the fish came because she respected them; she didn't walk through their lies or shout on a quiet night. She knew where to look to spot the subtle rises.

Dinks and whitefish, mostly, Layla said. They quit rising a while ago. I pulled an eighteen incher out of that seam off the bank, but that was right after we got here. Are you drunk?

Not yet, said RL. I wouldn't rule it out, though.

I'm going to go up to the house, said Layla.

Oh, sit with us a minute, said June. I haven't seen you since Christmas. How's college life?

* * *

Oh, you know, said Layla. Collegy.

Are you staying in the dorms next year?

Layla accepted her fate, laid her fly rod carefully against a tree and sat with them temporarily, cross-legged on the ground, ready to take flight.

Me and a couple of girlfriends got a place in Ballard, said Layla. Like a little house. I got a scooter to run back and forth to U-Dub, too, it's *très, très* cool until it rains.

It doesn't rain much in Seattle, does it?

It doesn't bother you as much as you might think. I mean, jeez, it can't be worse than February around here. At least the sun breaks through once in a while. No ice-fog.

Don't remind me, RL said. It's never going to be winter again.

June said, How's your love life?

I don't know, said Layla. How's yours?

And this just came out of her mouth so bitter and mean that it shut them all up. June had found a sore spot but RL didn't know what it was. This wasn't the kind of secret that Layla would ever share with him. It confused him, it made him sad the way that women were so closed to him. She was his daughter, his love, and yet a mystery.

Layla sprang to her feet in one lovely motion.

* * *

I'm really thirsty, she said. I'll see you up at the house.

She gathered her fly rod and left at once, a trail of negative ions in her wake. She hadn't meant to blurt this out, RL thought, but once it was said, it could not be unsaid, and after that none of them knew what to do.

When Layla was out of sight, June said, I'm so sorry. I didn't mean to put her on the spot.

It wasn't your fault, said RL. She's been half impossible all summer.

Something's going on with her.

Your guess is just as good as mine, said RL.

Has she seen her mom since she's been back?

Not that I know of. She wouldn't necessarily tell me. Dawn and I have been in kind of a bad patch lately.

Is she talking to anybody at all?

RL felt a familiar unease rise in his chest, almost an anger. He knew perfectly well that he wasn't enough of a father to Layla, or father and mother combined. People had been letting him know this since she was in the seventh grade and her mother had run off with a wildlands firefighter named Parker. There was no way to be right about this. He had stuck it out with Layla, had gone to the choir concerts and parent-teacher conferences, had taught her what he could of how to be a person. Yet every woman in the world let him know that he would never be enough. RL accepted this but he did not wish to be reminded of his failures. He had not forgotten them.

June didn't press. RL's cigar had gone out and he lit it again in a fat cloud of smoke, took the square bottle of Johnnie Walker and sipped at it. They had done this once all together—him and Dawn, Taylor and June. Before Layla came at all. Again he felt that smooth sadness in his chest, for Taylor gone, for Layla, for lonely June and the promise they had all felt there together by the river. They were going to be happy, they were going to adventure and live long and have stories to tell. Instead, he was living the same story over and over. Taylor was gone, Dawn was so unhappy that her eyes crossed from the pressure of it. Only Layla, the shy star . . . RL really did love her. There was comfort in that.

Comfort also in the blue glow of the summer sky, the light finally starting to extinguish, the red glow of his cigar when he drew on it—like a red bumblebee—and the moon trying to rise out of the trees, the two of them, him and June, striped and shifting with moon shadow. Really there was no place he wanted to be except right here.

Remember the time we drove up out of Great Falls heading for Glacier? RL said. Was that you that borrowed the convertible?

Don't, she said.

Don't what?

I'm going to stop doing this, she said.

RL heard it but he didn't really hear it. All that time he had been thinking one thing and she had been thinking something completely different. He blinked the smoke out of his eyes and said, What do you mean?

This is the last time for me, June said. I'm not coming back next year. Taylor was a beautiful man but he's dead.

I know that, RL said. Don't you think I know that?

Well, I didn't. Not till a little while ago. Like you were saying before, Robert, I would turn a corner and expect him to be there, you know? I'd go to bed at night and half expect to find him lying there. Wake up in the middle of the night, hugging my pillow and dreaming it was him. I'm done with that.

He couldn't read her face in the gathering dark but he saw the way she put her hand up to her throat, a thing she did when she was sad or troubled. He said, You can't just be done.

I can, she said. I am.

Like turning off a faucet.

No, she said. No, it's not like that at all. It's just, you know, like water on rock. It takes a while but . . . You just wake up one morning and it's not there anymore. I mean, I'm not going to stop remembering him. I'm not going to stop loving him.

No.

But I am going to stop acting like he's still here. Like he's going to walk through the door and everything's going to be OK.

You haven't been like that, RL said. He could feel something slipping away between them and he didn't want it to. He said, You've got your work, your friends.

Oh, crap, she said. I've been practicing this in my head for a week and I know it isn't going to come out right. Anyway. You're a good man and you've been a good friend to me and I've needed you, you know that. You've always been around when I needed you. But, Christ, Robert, you've got Layla and Dawn and what's her name; you've got your business; you've got your friends and your trips to New Orleans and wherever else—you're a busy man. I sleep alone, Robert, almost every night. More than you want to know, I know that, but still. I'm going to die and I know it, not too long from now, maybe, and I'm going to die alone because everybody does. But I don't want to live alone.

I'm sorry, RL said.

No, see that's not it! You've got nothing to be sorry about— you're a good man, Robert! I know I'm not saying this right. It's all mixed up in my mind.

They relapsed into silence then, water over rocks, a breeze in the leaves of the cottonwoods.

Cigarette, she said.

He lit one off the ash of his cigar and handed it to her.

* * *

RL felt like this was not happening, an unreal moment. Anger was rising in him but he didn't know why or at who. Not June. Maybe himself, who had failed again somehow. He didn't see how. He had never meant to be enough to her, but now he saw that he was not. He had put his shoulder to the wheel but it was not enough.

Whiskey, RL said, and she passed him the bottle.

June said, People die from not seeing the night sky, don't you think?

They don't die from it.

They die inside, and they don't even know it.

But they don't die from it. They just get numb.

Not me, she said. She reached over and took the bottle from his hand, then stood up from the rock and waded out into the water. RL flinched as he saw the cold water lap against her bare thighs, feeling a little sympathetic testicular cringe of his own. He didn't know what she was doing. She was being dramatic, and she was not a dramatic woman.

Here you are, said June. I am officially letting it go. All of it. I'm nobody's widow anymore.

She unstoppered the bottle and poured the whiskey that was left into the river, where it disappeared into the water, easily half a bottle. She held it over the water until the last drop was gone. RL felt like he was the one being left behind. She was saying good-bye to him. He didn't know if he was right or wrong, but his heart balled up in his chest and he wanted to stop her. *Don't go,* he wanted to say. *Stay here with me. It'll be all right.*

But he didn't say anything. When the last of the whiskey was gone, she put the stopper back in the bottle and for a moment she wanted to throw it, he could see that. In the end she didn't. She was not a dramatic person at heart and would not want to scatter broken glass around the riverside just to make a point. Somebody could get hurt. She held onto the bottle instead and came up dripping out of the water and kissed RL, which surprised him. Usually she didn't. He stood into her embrace and felt her shiver in the night air.

It's going to be all right, she said softly, like he was a baby, like RL was the one who needed comforting. She said, It's going to be fine.

But inside his mind, RL just didn't know.

*

Layla left her fly rod on the porch of June's house and went inside. The front door was unlocked as ever. The house was a ten-minute walk from the river across a hayfield that smelled of sweet grass, and outside was the last fading edge of twilight. She could see fine to follow the path, under the last blush of day and the emerging stars. But when she went inside and turned on the lights, it turned into solid black night outside the windows.

The dinner dishes sat on the table, corncobs and steak bones. Layla would do the dishes in a minute, would save the bones for Rosco, June's old golden. In a minute she would let Rosco in from the pen out back.

First she went back into the bedroom, where June kept her computer, to see if there was any word from Russia. It was eight thirty in the morning in St. Petersburg, tomorrow already. Daniel would be awake, unless he slept in. Alone, unless he wasn't. Layla knew she shouldn't worry but she did. There was no real reason, except that when she booted up her e-mail account, there was still nothing there and it had been two days. In a hotel room in Russia with a dozen other would-be poets. Daniel with his glossy brown hair and his deep, thoughtful eyes. What was it about her, that she couldn't just relax and trust him? (But what if it wasn't about her at all? What if it was something about him, something she knew and couldn't admit?)

Nineteen years old, barely qualified. Daniel was in graduate school.

Fuck, she said out loud. Fuck, fuck, fuck.

The word reverberated around the prim walls of the bedroom. June kept her house neat. A little fluffy and flowery like a girl's bedroom, lace on the bedside table, though there were books on the table, too, and a big practical light overhead. A surprising crowd of perfumes and powders on the dresser, a well-lit mirror above. June didn't look like that kind of woman—green grass and fresh air was her look, short practical hair—but Layla understood that it was never that simple. This whole house seemed to make a little too much sense, a little too orderly, almost fearful. June wasn't that way but she was almost that way, keeping the scary world away by cleanly magic. Layla realized while she was thinking this that she herself probably still had fish slime on her hands and she had touched the keyboard of June's computer, which, if past experience held, could in a day or so start to smell really, really rank.

* * *

Daniel was seven years older than Layla and 100 percent of everybody who knew about it hated the idea. He might be making a fool out of her at that very moment. Do people fuck around at eight thirty in the morning? If they are the kind of people who fuck around.

Layla let the old dog in and pressed her face to his neck, the soft, dog-smelling fur. Half dog, half rug, Rosco was content to be held. But there was a spark in his eyes when she picked the steak bones off the table, a puppyish alertness and wag. She teased him with the bones, then gave in. Let the dog get what he wants, anyway. Layla stood at the sink, up to her elbows in hot soapy water, and thought that she deserved whatever she got. Learn to protect yourself. Don't give yourself away like nothing, like a motel matchbook. Outside in the night, things were stirring, the bats and birds and owls. Once Layla saw five owls standing in the same dead tree, right down by the river, right by where June and her father were sitting. Field mice hunting for food, scampering for their lives. Talons first, the owl slashing down out of the night sky.

Me, the little field mouse, Layla thought.

Around her the house felt content, sleepy. Taylor and June had bought it derelict when they were first married, windows boarded up and mouse shit everywhere. Layla had seen the pictures: it was hard to believe. The bones of the house were good, is the way June said it: a stage station on the old Mullan Road, one of the first houses in the valley. It sat in a compound of long, pretty barns and beat-up houses for the hands, a tall cool willow tree in the yard. In the main barn, you could see the beams cut from the ponderosa pines that used to grow in the valley, seventy-foot spans out of a single timber. Some of the tall trees still grew here, not many. The new crap houses were creeping up on all sides.

Doing the dishes, trying not to think about Russia, feeling the quiet all around her.

June and Taylor fixed this place up themselves, with their own hands. That was the story, anyway. Sometimes Layla felt like she didn't have a childhood or a history but just a bunch of stories that she had to piece together for herself. She never knew what was true or at least what was the whole truth. The two of them on nights and weekends and vacations out here painting and plastering. RL and Taylor up on the roof, nailing cedar shakes on a summer evening. RL and Dawn, happy together on the porch. The house-wrecking party, when they decided to tear down one of the old tenant shacks to open up the yard. June and Taylor invited everybody they knew to come bring a wrecking bar or a sledgehammer, and they tore it down and lit it on fire, had chicken and beer and a live band. Was Layla there? She didn't have any definite memory but she thought she remembered a big fire, shouts and laughter, the firemen standing by. . . .

Maybe it was just a dream—sometimes her thoughts came alive while she was sleeping, and something she was told, or something she read in a book, would live in her mind as a memory after the dream had come and gone. A real memory, one she could touch. The heat of the fire on her face, the smoke and beer. She asked her mother once, and two of the three first things from her life that she thought she remembered never happened at all. Or maybe Dawn just forgot. Or maybe Layla made it all up. There was no place real, nothing she could touch, just dreams and memories and wanting things. Just now she wanted Daniel.

She would ask her father, when he came back from the river, if the house-wrecking party had been real. She was almost sure it was. Almost.

*

When they were gone, June sat alone in her kitchen. She had certainly fucked things up. She had hurt him. From somewhere, some safe place, she felt a desire to hurt herself in recompense. She wouldn't do it. But she could picture it: getting the knife out of the knife block where it slept, scalpel sharp, the feel of the cool steel on her skin and the surprising ease of a sharp blade . . . She wouldn't. She sat at the table half drunk and all smoked out and sick of herself. Why couldn't she just be easy? Take the love she was given.

Her old dog slept at her feet. She poured a glass of white wine from the box in the fridge. It was eleven thirty and she had to be up at seven for work, but she knew she wouldn't sleep. Her clothes didn't fit her and her hair was somebody else's, somebody old and tired. This old house fit over her like a shell, like a snake's skin, something she needed to split, to crack, to grow out of. To smash, to vomit, to cut, to tear. June was stuck.

Rosco looked up at her. Then he laid his threadbare head to rest on the kitchen floor again and heaved a long pleasurable sigh.

When he was gone, June would sell the place. She'd do it now except that the move would kill him. He'd never lived anywhere else, didn't know a thing about cars or mean dogs. He'd gotten into a tussle or two when the neighbors had a border collie, but he was big enough to hold his own. Never anything bad except the time he got into the chickens. Chasing deer a few times. It was strange to think that Rosco was a killer at heart, a pack animal, chasing baby deer, circling, killing. One time, she was almost sure. Maybe two. Out killing in the night.

When Rosco was gone she'd move into town, someplace with some life to it, someplace with human noise. Here it was the refrigerator clicking on and off, the wind in the eaves, her own soft footsteps on the painted fir floor. She finished her wine in one long sip and started for bed. Then June realized that she still had no chance of sleep, not yet. She stood in her kitchen, between her seat at the table and the refrigerator, trying to decide whether to pour herself another glass of wine. She stood nearly paralyzed. It was not a decision that mattered at all, but still she could not make it. All alone and paralyzed in the middle of everything: the night, her life, her kitchen.

After a minute she poured herself another glass of wine after all and sat back down at the kitchen table. June thought to herself, I am just sitting here waiting for the dog to die.

*

In August RL and Edgar floated a stretch of the Bitterroot to see if it could be done. It hadn't rained in six weeks and the irrigators had been sucking the life out of the thing to keep the hayfields green. The river braided through banks of gravel, river bottom when there was water to cover them but desert now. The sight of it made RL angry. He loved this river despite all its treachery and deceit and now it had been insulted, shrunken.

Edgar was a guide from RL's shop, twenty years younger and just out of graduate school in art. He was a painter, thin and sharp-featured, quick hands. His instincts were impeccably sharp for fish. Next to him, RL felt fat and old and slow, all of which he was— Oliver Hardy to Edgar's Stan Laurel. Edgar was supposed to take a couple of clients down on the next morning, and so him and RL went on an evening float just to take a look. They brought a half case of beer on ice in RL's oldest and worst raft, a no-name Tai-wanese special that had already been patched in twelve places. If they had to drag a boat, this was the one to drag. They started drinking beer as soon as the boat pushed off from the ramp, about four o'clock on a hot, sunny, smoky afternoon. Big forest fires were burning down by Darby and back in the Selway, and the valley was filling up with smoke like a cup full of dirty milk. The far mountains were gone in a gray-brown haze.

Gorilla, Edgar said from the oarsman's seat.

No way, said RL.

African lowland gorilla.

RL paused to cast, a big foam ant with a San Juan worm on a dropper. This was the laziest and most degenerate kind of fishing there was, sitting in a chair on a boat with a cold beer in his hand, casting big junk at the bank and letting the river carry them along. All he was lacking was a cigar and he had plans for one.

RL said, You ever see a grizzly bear up close?

Up in Glacier, sure.

From a mile away, RL said. With a ranger standing next to you with a high-powered rifle in his hand.

A little closer than that.

I was fishing the White River one time, RL said, right back in the middle of the Bob. I was standing in the river, wet wading, and I just got that weird eyes-in-the-back-of-my-head feeling, you know, like I could feel something was watching me.

A grizzly bear.

Right on the bank, said RL. Big as a boxcar.

What did you do?

He was gone before I could even shit my pants, RL said. Just turned and ran. If I ever thought about trying to outrun one of those things, I don't think so anymore.

Fast.

Like a racehorse fast. I'm serious—he was gone before I even started to get scared, but once I did, I stayed scared. I mean, I didn't stop till I got back to my car. I don't know why he ran like that, either. It wasn't like he was scared of me.

Probably got a whiff of you.

It's true, RL said. A couple of nights of sleeping on the ground and my man-smell gets rolling pretty good.

He was talking to Edgar but his eyes were on the fly as ever, floating just off the bank. He hadn't seen a riser yet. That didn't matter so much with a fat attractor like the foam ant. In his peripheral vision he watched for cover, a stump or log or overhanging bush, that might conceal a fat trout. He was healthy and vigorous and doing what he liked to do, but when he thought about that bear, something inside him went weak and liquid still. A power radiated from the bear like light or heat. It didn't even matter, the claws and teeth and speed and size. The real power was something else, invisible.

The ant disappeared and RL set the hook immediately, feeling the tug of a live thing on the other end, the flash of silver turning brown in the green water. A fifteen incher, maybe sixteen, had taken the worm. A rainbow. RL worked it quickly toward the boat, horsing it in. The water was warm, this time of year, and the fish couldn't fight like they did in October. He brought it to the gunwale and wet his hand and lifted it briefly, just a moment to get the fly out. Then the fish was gone, back to its watery depths, its silvery light. Thank you, RL thought, a small automatic gesture like a baseball player crossing himself before an at-bat. He didn't know who he was thanking except he knew that he himself had not made this river. There was such a thing as grace. RL felt it.

Try something yellow, Edgar said.

Why?

I don't know, it was working the other day. Something big and hairy and yellow.

Madame X.

Sure.

RL tied the big ugly bug on obediently. RL himself knew the sequence of hatches on this river as well as anybody and could tie a decent imitation, but there were also times when nothing much was going on and that was where Edgar had him beat. His hunches were golden.

The thing about a gorilla, Edgar said, a gorilla is *smart*.

So what? Smart doesn't count for much when the freight train hits you.

They use tools.

Smart doesn't matter, RL said. Instinct is what counts. I'm smart as hell when I'm sitting in the store or reading a book, but when I'm out here, I'm not as smart as a fucking fish most of the time. Fish's brain is just a wide spot in its spinal column, but you put it in the environment, it knows everything it needs to know.

Put that grizzly bear in Africa, Edgar said.

It would still kick that monkey's ass.

Just then the water swirled around the yellow fly, and then he set the hook and felt the weight of it and then the reel started spinning out that high beautiful note he loved.

That's a nice fish, said Edgar.

RL didn't say anything, just palmed the rim of the spool to slow him down a little. Even on 3X he wasn't going to horse this one in. A big fish, maybe a very big fish. At first he thought it was a brown, but then—thirty feet away—it leaped from the water and spun in the air, a big beautiful rainbow shining bright in the afternoon sun. RL kept the rod tip up, to keep pressure on him, as he leaped and leaped again. RL started singing his little happy song to himself under his breath, the little music that he heard when he had a big fish on the line, maybe a very big fish, and the reel was holding and then he was gaining a few inches at a time. Happy little song, an inch at a time, and then the wild run when the thing took flight, the fly line knifing through the water and then the slow, slow retrieve and then . . .

RL stared at the slack fly line. The thing was gone.

The music died down right away. RL reeled in until he saw the place where the knot had parted, the tiny pitiful corkscrew of tippet, right where the fly had been tied on. This was his fault.

Dumbass, RL said.

Edgar didn't say a word, just pulled the anchor rope to set them moving again and took up the oars. Nothing for him to say except to agree with the dumbass comment, which wouldn't do. RL would fire his ass. He would hire him back the next day but still. RL could feel the memory of the thing in the muscles of his forearm, the weight and spunk. The boat was in the current now, drifting down past fishy banks, shady shallows and undercut root balls. He cut the twisted tippet off and tied a new fly on cleanly, checking his work this time, tugging on the fly, looking to make sure the knot was tidy and sure on the eye of the hook. He dressed the fly with Gink and flung it into the water again although he didn't want to. He didn't want to catch a different fish. He wanted to catch the one he had just lost, the big one.

* * *

After a hundred yards of river had passed, Edgar said, The important thing is just getting out.

RL decided to laugh at this rather than kill him.

Fresh air, he said. It's good for you.

RL lit his cigar then and they floated on, Edgar sometimes pulling on the oars to keep them lined up with the bank but mostly letting the current carry them downriver. A kingfisher followed them for a while, chattering loudly, and then RL spotted a beaver. He opened a cold beer. Any fish that came to him would be a sad little fish, he thought, and no match for the one that took his fly. But when he caught one and then another, he thought they were cheerful little fighters and the sight of them made him happy.

Then they came to an irrigation dam that stretched the full width of the river. Nobody knew for certain, but the rumor was that it fed the grass at Huey Lewis's place, either that or the golf course at the Stock Farm, a walled-in development with a Western theme and million-dollar lots. The dam itself was rocks and boulders piled into a wall, and what water was left, after the golfers took theirs, spilled over the top. The drop was four or five feet. Edgar stood up at the oars, trying to get a look at the curl of water, trying to judge the depth of the pool below.

You think we can make it? he asked RL.

Beats me.

You see a better way around it?

* * *

Get out and walk, RL said. Unload the boat and drag it across.

That doesn't sound like much fun.

Buckle up, then, RL said. I'll run a strap around the dry bag and the cooler. You drown my cigar you're going to pay for it.

I'll take my chances, Edgar said, and sat down to the oars again. RL tied everything down and then resumed his throne in the front of the boat. A nice excitable quiet before the dam. The air was warm and thick with smoke, a campfire smell. A blue heron watched them from the shallows of an inside bend. The pool above the dam was slow and still and they drifted calmly toward the lip of the drop. Then they were in it.

The front of the boat with RL in it launched off horizontally into the air at first, a strange dizzy sensation as the water dropped away and the rubber raft sagged beneath his feet. Then the central part of the boat with Edgar and the rowing frame went over the lip and the whole boat tipped forward at once, launching RL almost out of his seat and dropping fast. He managed to hold on to his fly rod as the ass end of the boat came round and over. They were going to make it over. They were going to make it until the ass end of the boat spun into the shallow edge and into a sharp rock, the rubber wedged between the rowing frame and the rock, and then a tearing sound and that quarter of the boat deflated at once, pitching the whole apparatus, baby and all, headfirst into the water.

It was deeper than RL thought and he had to dog-paddle out, half sideways, clutching his fly rod still. First things first. A moment of panic when he couldn't find bottom and he lost one of his sandals. Not here, he thought, not now, not me.

* * *

Then found himself wet and dripping on a gravel bank. He had no clear idea of how he had gotten there, but his waterlogged cigar was still pressed between his teeth and his fly rod was still in his grip. He was starting to laugh when he realized that he didn't see Edgar anywhere. The raft was still hung up on the rocks with water pouring through it and the tethered cooler flopping in the current. Behind him on either bank he didn't see a sign except Edgar's hat floating downstream. He looked again at the raft and saw a hand.

Edgar's hand was caught in the strap between the raft and cooler, back in deep water. When RL looked closer he could see Edgar's head through the curtain of water coming over the dam. He surfaced and tried to catch his breath, but the water pushed him back under. He fumbled with his free hand, trying to get loose. It was backward. The cooler was stuck between rocks, and it was the press of water against the raft that was holding him tight.

Without further thinking RL kicked his one sandal off and swam toward the boat. With the current against him it was slow going. He didn't have time. A white buzz like anger went off in his head. Fuck this river. Edgar had a young wife and a daughter and RL pictured them in his mind. He swam till he got there, somehow, shaking with the effort, his arms soft and sore. Then he was on the rocks and he didn't know what to do. He tried to pull the raft in, to take the grip off, but the press of water against it was more than his strength. Edgar was coming up and going under, coming up and going under. Then RL remembered.

He remembered the knife in his kit bag, which was where? Somewhere with the boat—he remembered strapping it to the rowing frame. RL ran his hand along the frame, under it and behind, blind, half underwater until his hand found the strap and drew it in and *there* was the bag and *there* the side pocket and *there* in the pocket was the knife, wicked sharp. He flicked it open one-handed and cut the strap and the whole assembly—raft, bag, Edgar and RL—drifted off the curl of the water. Sill hanging on to the raft frame, he saw that Edgar was free and half swimming on his own and so decided to bring the raft to shore if he could. RL drifted down until he felt gravel under his bare feet and then dragged the broken raft up onto the bank, the one quarter all deflated and flapping. He got it up into the weeds and looked upstream and saw Edgar safe on the bank, standing, holding his one arm with the other. A start of wind rustled through the cottonwoods, a sound of ease, and something triumphant started up in RL's chest. He had beaten it. RL started to laugh, picking his way barefoot through the rocks.

I think I broke my arm, Edgar said.

RL quit laughing when he saw the pale light of his face, blood empty.

How'd you do that?

I don't really know, Edgar said. It's kind of a blur. I'm going to sit down for a minute.

Does it hurt much?

Yes, it does.

* * *

Can you move it?

But this was more than Edgar could answer. He sat on the gravel and waved RL away, sat a little too hard, dizzy. A hot dry wind blew through the canyon then. Leaves rattled in the forest fire smoke.

*

Women were starving to death in the streets and
their bodies left to freeze on the sidewalk. They were eating the
rats, their pets, the animals from the zoo; they were eating each
other. The human butchery.

Layla put her book aside and sipped her lemonade. Something
was wrong with one of them, either her or Daniel. He came back
from Russia all lit up, everything about Russia, about the food and
the art, the women and the suffering. Over e-mail and long phone
calls—he had only made plans as far as Seattle, would not commit
to a trip to Montana—he told her what to read and which movies to
watch. So far she had made it through *Anna Karenina*, *Notes from
Underground* and *Solaris*. One of them was crazy, her or Daniel.
This book she was reading now, he insisted, all about the siege of
Leningrad and it was half military history and half pure suffering.

She could not understand his enthusiasm. Yes, it happened. No, it was not that long ago. But why? When she thought of him, it was lying in her bed in morning sunlight, legs in a furry angle, the glossy brown of his long hair. Not enough for Daniel, apparently. And he would not say definitely whether he was coming to see her, and it was only a day's drive away. . . .

It was near sunset. College would be starting in three weeks. She would see him then and everything would be settled. At least she would know. That little spark of fear at the thought of knowing. That taste of pennies.

Her cell phone rang and it was RL. He needed her to pick them up by the side of 93. There had been an accident. No, everybody was OK, or pretty much OK. The turnout just by Poker Joe.

But when she saw them, Layla knew that things were not OK. She recognized Edgar from the shop but she had never seen him so ghostly. The two of them like Mutt and Jeff by the side of the road, Edgar all tall and narrow and sharp-nosed—a bony man but elegant, assembled from wire hangers—and RL next to him in his solid flesh. My dad, she thought. The solid father. She still hated the beard and wondered if she might talk him out of it before she went back to college. But even solid RL looked confused, too many second thoughts in the way he moved, now this and now that. A boat's worth of crap by the sides of the road, cooler, dry bags, oars.

What's going on?

Had a little pileup on the river, RL said, bluff but unconvincing.

* * *

Is everybody OK?

Edgar here thinks he might have broke an arm.

I'm pretty sure, said Edgar. He wasn't complaining, but it wasn't a joke either.

She opened the door for him and he got in, cradling one arm with the other, and sat still, staring ahead, while they piled the gear into the back of the pickup. RL wouldn't even look at him and he wasn't talking to anybody. Edgar was pissed. When they were loaded up, RL stuffed himself into the jump seat behind Layla, where he didn't fit well. She could feel his giant bony knees in the small of her back.

Drop me at Chief Looking Glass, would you? RL asked. I've got to pick up the trailer and it's on the way. I'll meet you down at Saint Pat's.

Layla smelled stale beer and cigar smoke and rolled her window down an inch. She didn't want to, didn't want to, didn't want to. But she didn't want to have to back the trailer, either. Edgar sat beside her, radiating anger. What was it about men? If she stayed with Daniel long enough, would he turn into one of these? Would he smell of sweat and sunblock and beer? Would he scratch and bleed? RL liked to see a little of his own blood once in a while. He really didn't mind. Layla never understood this.

They let RL off to run the shuttle, and then it was just the two of them on the way to the hospital. Layla couldn't think of a single thing to say. It was going to be a half-hour drive from here at least.

* * *

How did this happen? she finally asked.

It was just dumbass, he said.

What kind?

Edgar told her about the wreck, then, and when he got to the part about being caught underwater with his hand tied down, Layla could tell how frightened he had been. Still was. He said, I didn't think I was going to get out of there.

He held a hand out, palm toward the windshield, as if to ward off the death angel; and out of the corner of her eye she noticed that he was graceful in his movements, like the arc of a good cast—she could feel it in her own body, when it worked. Grace.

Also the smell of sweat and beer and cigars was her father's. With him gone, the truck just smelled of river water.

RL is such an asshole sometimes, Layla said.

My fault more than his, Edgar said. I was sitting at the oars.

It just seems like this kind of crap always happens when he's *around*, you know? And it never happens to him, either. Always to the people around him, the lucky bastards.

Edgar laughed, then felt it in his broken arm. Out of the corner of her eye she saw him pale.

* * *

You got a mouth on you, he said.

So I've been told.

Did you grow up around RL the whole time?

Layla laughed. She said, You think there's a connection?

Could be.

Mostly I did, she said. When my mom first got back to town, she thought she wanted to try her hand at me. I went back and forth for a while till she left again.

Went where?

RL didn't tell you the story? He loves to tell this story. No, she ran off and followed the Grateful Dead around, years at a time. She used to sell hemp necklaces with rocks and beads and stuff.

Get out of here.

No, it's amazing.

I've only seen her that one time at the store.

No, she doesn't look the part at all anymore. Unless you see her with a sleeveless shirt—she's got this whole spiderweb tattooed on her shoulder and part of her arm. It's huge. It's actually kind of awesome.

* * *

Live and learn, said Edgar. They settled back into silence, but it was a companionable silence now. They were on the same side, though Layla didn't know of what. After a minute, Edgar started to laugh. He didn't explain himself, and she didn't ask why. She didn't need to. She already knew so much.

*

Later in the bar they had beer and cheeseburgers under a wall of photographs of grinning fishermen and women holding unbelievably large fish out in the air. RL was half drunk by then and he had to be up at five thirty in the morning to take the clients Edgar could not. So he ordered a Johnnie Walker on the rocks for himself and another for Edgar.

Who's going to drive you home? asked Layla.

I'm all right, RL said.

You might be out of luck for today, she said.

Out of *bad* luck, you mean. We used up all the bad luck. It's going to be sunshine and sweet peas from here on out.

* * *

RL sat back in his chair and watched the waitress's ass for a minute. He was being a dick and he knew it. But he felt obscurely that the other two were ganging up on him, a little vibe when he walked into the waiting room at Saint Pat's just as Edgar was coming out with his new cast. He should maybe have gotten there earlier.

But since RL's mother died, he hated hospitals, the stink of them, the machine quiet and hiss. Behind the politeness and soft voices lurked suffering and death. Her last ten days, when he slept in the waiting room, or in a chair in her room while she struggled for breath, RL sometimes took the elevator up to Labor and Delivery just to watch happiness, just to believe in it. Strolling the corridor, feeling like a spy—he didn't belong there, he had no business—RL strained to see the new mother through the half-open door, the little blanket-wrapped bundle, the older brother or sister with balloons or flowers, the sad exhausted husbands who were happy but something else at the same time, something nobody cared to name. . . . Even in the happy place, the other crept in. A kind of machinelike compassion, real, inadequate. As sorry as they all fucking were, his mother wasn't coming back.

Layla was drinking diet soda and looking beautiful and disapproving with her long beautiful neck until Edgar said something funny and then she liked him. His cast already looked dirty in the dim bar light. The waitress disappeared into the next room, tall and blond, a basketball player maybe. She had a high-set ass like a black woman and long muscular legs.

RL said, You can take the store, can't you?

* * *

Edgar said, Me?

It's wages work, RL said. Probably enough to keep you going for a while. You won't make what you make guiding.

No, I appreciate it. I'm not going to know what the hell I'm doing, though.

There's no great trick to it, RL said. The little ray of sunshine here can show you how to run the cash register et cetera.

There's not much to it, Layla said.

No, I do appreciate it. I was kind of counting on some of that money.

RL looked at him, his grateful kindly face, and suddenly he was done—done with the evening, done with the scene. Five in the morning loomed in front of him and the raft still half deflated by the side of the stream and clients to please, never his favorite part of the operation. The blond waitress with the beautiful ass was not going to sleep with him and this last glass of whiskey was not going to make anything better. He drained it, ice rattling his teeth, and threw sixty dollars at his daughter.

Settle up, he said, would you? I'm going to take a leak.

She was surprised by this turn of mood, he could see it in her face, her and Edgar. I am your father, RL thought, I disappoint you. That's what I do. That's my job. In the green toilet light his eyes like a wino, his fat gut bulging, his fishing shirt with the silly flaps and buttons. What was he trying to prove? The boy in him. Tying flies and rowing boats—a boy's idea of a man's life—and here he was with a daughter and all, circles under his eyes like fucking Rembrandt. Piss came slower and weaker always. He had managed to make a little money—fisherman and landlord—and keep his daughter alive. That was all. There were times when that seemed like enough, but here, alone in green light with his dick in his hand, it did not.

When he came back to the bar they were head down, talking. This wasn't exactly wrong, but it wasn't right. Change and check were already on the table, good to go.

I'll run the casualty home, RL said. Meet you back at the house.

I might go out for a while, Layla said.

Out where?

You know, *out*, Layla said. The other side of the door.

I don't like you out in the bars.

Which is exactly where we are right now, she said.

OK, OK, OK, he said. Just don't make a racket when you come in. I've got to be up early.

I'll bring the brass band, she said.

In the car, Edgar said, That girl's a ball of fire.

* * *

Sometimes, RL said. She feels comfortable with you, you see that side of her. She's a complicated girl, though, sometimes she just runs out of gas. She seems a lot older than she really is.

This was meant as a warning and Edgar heard it that way, maybe. He settled in his side of the truck and shut up for the ride back to his house. It was early but late, the streets just lining up with college drunks and Layla out there somewhere among them. RL had been awake since six and didn't understand why all the yelling, the drinking, the driving around in cars. Though he remembered the moment when the boat had tipped over the lip of the dam with a great pleasure. Dangerous fun. But fun.

What did you do?

Edgar's wife stood in the porch light like she wasn't going to let him in. A drooly little toddler girl watched from the living room behind her, scared. Then Amy turned to RL.

What did you do to him? she said. Why does this garbage always happen when he's out with you?

It's not his fault, Edgar said.

I didn't say it was, she said. You'd better come in.

She stood aside in the doorway and watched RL sideways and angry. He wasn't fooling her. Edgar inside with his daughter in his arms and then Amy closed the door on him and RL was alone on the porch. He could hear the fight starting up behind the closed door. A nice night, finally cooling off, insects buzzing in the shadows and RL alone again. The yellow light of the living room spilled out onto the lawn, warm—a promise of family, a life inside, a place to go.

He made his way back to the truck and drove to his own empty house. The message light was blinking red on the telephone but RL ignored it in favor of one last beer on the deck. And possibly a cigar. Definitely a cigar. He'd pay for it in the morning, but he couldn't sleep right now anyway. RL was restless, restless. The town spread out below him, a bowl full of lights, headlights, streetlights, little lights spilling from warm little houses and always the cars on their way to somewhere. Who was that on the phone? RL didn't really want to know. He sat back and watched the lights and sipped his beer and watched the late Northwest flight out of Minneapolis line up on the airport across the valley, miles away. The runway lit up as the plane approached, twinkling in the night air. He lit his cigar and sat back in his lawn chair to watch. Man, drink, deck, summer night, cigar.

RL took a basic pleasure in big engines, jets and graders and locomotives, a pleasure that was carried over from his Ohio boyhood. He used to take Layla to the overpass at the north end of town and together watch the trains underneath their feet, sometimes feeling the diesel heat, the clangor of boxcars run together, the screech of metal brakes. Something about him that women didn't trust, that they didn't like exactly. It wasn't just the broken bones, the trouble that followed him. It wasn't the guilty fact of him sitting with a drink in his hand at midnight when he had to be up at five, the toy pleasure of watching the big jet land across the way. They still flew the old three-engine 727s in and out of the valley, one of the last places they could fly them, too noisy for almost anyplace else, but they could punch through an inversion layer like nobody's business.

No, it was something else they didn't trust, something intangible. The fact that he liked this day, that he felt alive in the face of it. Something happened, nobody died. Boredom was held at bay. Mission accomplished. Not a woman alive, at least none RL had met, would have followed this logic. Maybe they were right. Maybe let the women run the world for a change, if they weren't already. But RL felt a deep conviction that he was right about this. Prudence could be carried only so far before it became cowardice, and cowardice was a dead end.

He looked forward to explaining this position to Edgar's wife.

Across the valley, the 727 followed the bright beams of its landing lights down, a long shallow glide that circled the valley and then straightened in alignment with the runway. He could barely hear the big motors. Then touchdown, all safe, a kind of inner thrill.

Then the phone rang again and he went and looked at the caller ID: his ex-wife, Dawn, calling at midnight. RL did not know much, but he did know well enough to leave this call for another day. The women of the world would have to find somebody else to pick on tonight. He was done with errands, done with explanations. If this was an emergency, it was not his emergency. He took a bottle of Trout Slayer from the fridge, in case the first one ran out, and went back outside to watch the lights, to feel the summer, fading fast. After a minute, the phone began to ring again, and he let it.

*

Nothing good will come of this, June thought. Nothing good ever came of a man with a clipboard or a mustache or a big hat, and Howard Emerson had all three.

Funny thing, he said. They were striding through cut hay, walking the back fence line where it ran up next to the state park. June could smell the river, late summer, low water, muck and rot. They were right by the water.

Bunch of hippies back in I think it was 1969, Howard Emerson said. Borrowed money from Mom and Dad and I don't know who or what-all else and they got together and bought six hundred acres down on Kootenai Creek and started a hippie commune, the real thing. It didn't last long. I guess they all hated each other by the end, plus there was some random shooting and so on by the locals.

That was back when the Posse Comitatus was in action—you ever hear of them?

No, said June.

Make the Freemen look like a Sunday-school outfit, said Howard Emerson. Anyway, they got run out of there—or they run themselves out, whichever—and I guess none of 'em could stand each other enough to talk to one another. The place just sat the same as you're doing, leasing out the hay and renting out the house. Thirty years of this. Then one of 'em died, I guess, and they called me up to put a value on the place. None of 'em had any idea. They about fell down when I gave them the number. Jim Canady lives there now.

He looked at her under the brim of his hat like she was supposed to be impressed, but June drew a blank.

Baseball pitcher, said Howard Emerson. Middle relief, setup guy. Threw for the Cardinals for a while. Nicest person you ever met.

Great! she said.

Bunch of rich hippies now, said Howard Emerson. Ex-hippies, I guess, by now. Just goes to show.

What does it go to show? June wanted to know. *To whom does it show what? To whom? Who tomb? No more of Howard Emerson for me.*

I'm not making you nervous, am I? asked Howard Emerson.

* * *

No, no.

You seem nervous.

No, I . . .

I guess you've had this place for a while, he said. Must have been pretty nice out here. You got in before the golf course. I remember it used to stink out here something awful from the paper mill. Glad they got that business cleaned up. Just like a wet dog, all day and all of the night. Don't know how you could stand it.

It was never that bad.

Oh, yes it was. I remember. But, you know, all's well that ends well. I imagine you got the place for a pretty good price. I'm not going to ask but I imagine it was a good, good price. I think you'll be pretty pleased if you do decide to sell.

I haven't really made up my mind yet, June said. I keep going back and forth.

I absolutely understand.

A lot of memories tied up in one place.

I'm not trying to talk you into anything, one way or the other, said Howard Emerson. I'm just saying. You don't have to leave the memories behind with the place—you can take them with you, whatever you decide. Hell, I grew up in California, in a place that's not even there anymore. The same houses and the same streets but nobody even speaks English now. And it's a nice neighborhood, too, still a nice neighborhood, it's just full of people from the Philippines. But, you know, none of it goes away—we've all got the pictures and the memories. A lot of us still keep in touch.

June didn't believe him. June thought he sounded wishful, like he was trying to talk himself into something. Time *annihilates*, she thought. Something is there and then it isn't there anymore. My mother is gone, she thought, my father, my husband. This is what time *does*. This is how it works. She was not so much angry at Howard Emerson as angry in general at the workings of the world, the continual theft and promise.

A bright clear afternoon, anyway, with a few high hazy clouds. It was not autumn yet but it would be soon. Back to school, back to life. They walked through the dry tall grass at the edge of the hayfield and back toward the house, Howard first in his tall hat and his big waterproof boots, June following in her long skirt. She felt ladylike and landed as she had wanted to, an Englishwoman in the West. Maybe she would offer him tea when they got back to the house. Maybe she would toss him out. But she had invited him in the first place, a friend of a friend who could tell her ballpark what the place was worth, and English ladies do not throw out their guests. She would make him tea, and watch him filter it through his enormous mustache.

August, afternoon, lemonade, dresses. Tennis. The mood made her nostalgic, remembering high school, her own long legs.

In the front hall, though, in the big mirror, in her sporty sandals and short practical hair, she thought she looked like a lesbian, one of the outdoor cheerful practical lesbians she knew from the hospital. So much for the mood. She offered him beer, which he declined, and then lemonade, which he took. A glass of white wine for herself. When they went inside, Howard Emerson took off his hat, and immediately shrunk, not just the inches the hat gave him but half his girth and stature. The top of his head was white and soft as a baby's ass and his mustachio loomed enormous, out of place. June had a vision, first the hat and then the boots and then the coat and jeans, by the time you got him naked there would be nothing left, a tiny larva.

Do you want to know? he said.

They sat at the dining room table, afternoon sunlight across the wood floors and a little breeze to ruffle the curtains. Old appraisals and tax records and plats between them.

Why wouldn't I?

It might change the way you feel about things. Might make things harder.

I doubt it, June said.

All right, then.

He shuffled the papers on the table in front of him and pursed his lips. When he looked up again he was a little angry, a little sharp. He had tried to be understanding and she had spurned him.

Two and change, he said. Two-two, maybe two-three.

Two million dollars.

* * *

Two million two hundred thousand dollars, he said. Could go a little higher, as I say, and it might go for less but I doubt it. There are not so many parcels this size left in the valley. Thank God for Hoerner Waldorf, right? You held on through the stink of it, when nobody else wanted to live out here.

It was never that bad, she said again, but this time dreamlike, an automatic repetition. She was dazed by the prospect of money. The places she could go, the shoes she could buy, the time, the days unending to herself . . . June touched the papers on the table, like the magic was contained in them. Howard Emerson was watching her. There was a person behind those blue eyes, she saw it all at once. A person. This came as a surprise. Not a doctor, not a predator. June kept her distance, fed her fear, but thought now that there was maybe nothing to be afraid of. His eyes looked kind and tired and they looked directly into her own.

That's a bit of luck, she said.

Good luck, bad luck, he said gently. It's all fine until you've got to pay property taxes on it.

I don't mind paying taxes.

Howard didn't believe her.

No, really, she said. She didn't know why but it felt important to explain herself. She said, Schools and sidewalks and firemen, I'm all for them. As long as everybody's paying their share.

Scolding and earnest, even to her own ears. Would you like to see my Birkenstocks?

* * *

Howard didn't seem to mind, or even notice. He said, That's the only thing, you know—there's nothing wrong with just sitting on the place, I mean, it's not going to go down in value and it seems like it works for you. There's no real reason. But, you know, the neighbors get together and put through an SID, or you get reappraised. I'm just saying that other people might end up making this decision for you.

You're the Devil, aren't you?

Howard Emerson seemed startled.

Come to tempt me with the whole wicked world, she said.

I'm just trying to keep myself in Cokes and pizza, he said. Keep the horses in oats. I don't know anything about the wicked world.

What kind of horses?

Nothing fancy, said Howard Emerson. Basically I'm running an old folks' home for horses. Or maybe like a bar, you know, a bunch of old guys sitting around shooting the breeze. I like them fine but they're no good for anything.

This seemed to June to ask as many questions as it answered but she didn't want to press. Besides, she had other fish to fry. Would she be rich? It was like somebody had asked to marry her, and now she had to decide. Howard Emerson, she thought. The Devil himself. What would baby Jesus do?

*

Layla dreamt of that apartment where the soldiers found the butchery, the headless disembodied corpses, the knives, the fat sleek butchers with their pink skin. . . . She knew one of the dead, she didn't know why. Ghostly she watched, like a camera in the corner, an eye and nothing more. Like a Picasso, she thought, *Picasso, Picasso, Picasso.* The word was still repeating in her head when she woke, disassembled and senseless. She could taste it in her mouth, gray-blue and brown. Bitter Picasso. The very end of summer.

*

RL regards the telephone. It rings again. It is his ex-wife on the line, the ex-wife who has left him five messages in three days, none of which say more than *Call me.*

Eventually he will have to answer, but he can't think of any reason it has to be now.

He doesn't like to talk to her. He doesn't like to lie, and he lies whenever he talks to her—not even about consequential things, about the small stuff, the everyday, even about Layla. RL finds Dawn confusing and difficult, and he doesn't want her in his life. It's not even that he hates her—it would be simpler if he did—but instead he feels this basement mess of emotions: pity and exasperation and sometimes even nostalgia for a life, a partnership and dream that they never actually had. A yard sale of a feeling, stuff he hasn't thought about in forever and doesn't want and now he has to do something about it. She should have a nice life if she wanted one. RL was fine with that. He just wished that she would have her nice life somewhere else—in Hawaii, for instance, where she actually went for a couple of years, making his life easy.

Dawn is not about making his life easy.

The telephone stops ringing, and then starts again. It's her again. He loved her once, he must have. They made this miracle child together. Where did that feeling go? When did she become this pure and holy pain in the ass?

Hello, he said.

Robert, Dawn said. I've been calling and calling.

My phone was broken, he lied. I didn't even know!

Have you heard about Betsy? she asked.

RL fought the urge to disconnect. This could only be the preface to bad news, Dawn's favorite subject.

What about her?

Well, it's back.

What do you mean, *back*?

* * *

I guess she was having some neck pain or something, Dawn said. She went to the clinic up in Bigfork and I guess they found something when they did the X-ray.

A kind of glee in her voice that repulsed RL like a sickness, which it was. This was the real dope, the inside information.

So I guess she's coming down on Monday for some more imaging, Dawn said, and I was wondering if she could stay with you.

How come?

Well, she needs a place to stay. The night before and then after—she doesn't want to drive all the way back up the valley in the dark. Plus, she has a follow-up the next day.

No, he said, I understand that part. But why me?

I'll be honest with you, Dawn said—which was the noise she made when she was getting ready to uncork some whopper. She said, That last time, when she had all the trouble, she was just such a negative force, you know? All that negative energy—I just don't have room for that in my life right now. I'm just barely keeping my head above water right now, Robert, I'm just worried and worried.

But I'll be OK with it.

You don't let these things affect you so much, Robert. You don't feel them the same way.

Thanks.

* * *

You know what I mean.

He knew exactly what she meant: an insensitive oaf who trod through life on a path of other people's feelings. That's me! he thought. And also: Fuck you!

But he didn't say it.

Which is how RL found himself staring out the window at a night full of rain in just-September, waiting for the headlights. He was sitting in his dining room alone. It was around eight o'clock. The rain had come on late in the evening and RL had not bothered to turn on the lights, so now he sat in twilight, listening to the rain. Layla was out someplace and soon she would be gone to Seattle again, back to college. He was at home in this blue light, dripping and dark. Alone in the dark. These last weeks had been among people, out running rivers with clients, meeting with prospective tenants for his rental houses—the public and RL the public servant. RL needed the quiet, the time alone. Soon Layla would be back in Seattle and he would get his quiet in spades.

He knew he ought to get up and turn the lights on, just so it looked like somebody was home, but he didn't.

He didn't stir until he heard her Toyota pickup rattle dead in the driveway. A faint feeling of being caught. This was not what he wanted Betsy to know about him, this sitting alone in the dark. A man of feeling, a man of action. It took him a minute to get going, reluctant.

Hey, she said. How *are* you?

* * *

He had forgotten her accent, still faintly Tennessee. In the porch light, she looked beautiful. He had forgotten this, too: the delicate lines of her face, her dark smooth skin. She was tall, almost as tall as RL. In one hand she held a Mason jar of something clear and gripped the handles of a giant many-colored basket in the other, like she was running away from home. She rushed to embrace him, and the basket whacked him in the back.

Look at you, she said. Sitting all by yourself in the dark.

How are you?

I don't know, she said, and grinned. I don't think I'm too good, but we'll know more tomorrow.

She came inside as ever with her basket and jar and several other bags and bundles. She moved through life in the middle of her own rummage sale, surrounded by rummage. Some of it was knitting, some of it was food.

She handed the Mason jar to RL and said, I brought you moonshine whiskey.

Excellent, he said. Am I going to die from this?

If you drink the whole thing, you will. A shot or two won't hurt you.

They sat at the dining room table and RL brought them shot glasses and bottles of beer. Normally he preferred American trash beer in cans but Betsy would like this better, made locally with natural ingredients. *Fancy* beer.

* * *

Not too much for me, said Betsy as he poured her a shot. Not too much for you, either, if you know what's good for you. This stuff will have you barking at the moon.

Where'd you find it?

I'm not supposed to say.

They touched shot glasses and RL downed his clear whiskey in one take. It ran down his throat like gasoline jelly and set him to coughing, coughing hard enough so he had to stand up, let the air back in. Something, the whiskey or the lack of air, went to his head right away and he saw tiny rockets in his vision and floating bright spots.

Jesus, Mary and Joseph, RL said.

I warned you, said Betsy, and sipped hers ladylike.

Well, yeah, but you could of *told* me, he said. So what's going on?

He sat down again across from her and watched her face as she decided what to tell him and how. The fall's cold rain fell into the bushes outside, hissed into the grass and ran down the sidewalks. It was a night to be inside and now that Betsy was here, RL was glad of the company. This was not a night to be alone. The burning in his throat became heat in his belly and slowly spread outward into his arms and thighs and head.

I don't know, Betsy said. I don't really want to talk about it.

* * *

You look good.

No, I feel fine. I get up every morning at quarter to five and I go out and I milk my goats and then I get the kids off to school and then I go for a run. I take care of myself. I feel great. I eat right off the bottom of the food chain.

RL tinked his shot glass against the jar of whiskey and said, I'm glad to hear this is good for you.

You know what I mean.

I do, he said. It's not fair.

That's not it, she said. I got over that idea last time. Nothing's fair.

She stopped talking and looked so forlorn and blue that RL wanted to take care of her, to make her soup or tuck her in a comforter. He felt her weight, then, the way a body gets so suddenly heavy when it goes limp. Her weight was handed to him.

Are you hungry? RL asked.

You know what it is? Betsy said. I'm sorry, I should just be quiet. This is so much more than you need from me. It's so nice of you to put me up. To put up with me.

Tell me, RL said. What's going on?

* * *

She took a moment, took a sip of whiskey, shuddered at the taste and burn, pulled herself together again. The skin of her face was windblown and rough, a life in the open. Her face was pretty still, but her hands were like his hands, battered and wrinkled and spotted. Our hands give us away, he thought, always.

Everything I know, she said. Everything I believe about the universe tells me that intention is everything, you know? Eyes on the prize. You look at where you want to go and don't worry about where you might end up if you screw up completely. And, you know, my goats, my kids, my place, I've been living *one hundred percent* like I was going to be around. I've been clear about this, Robert. I've been like one hundred percent single mind. I know what I want and I want it completely and I'm absolutely clear about it.

Stuff happens, RL said. That last time, you didn't bring it on yourself. It wasn't your fault.

No, it wasn't my fault, Betsy said. But there was a lot of negative energy in my life at that point.

RL just looked at her with a fearful creepy feeling in his heart. Betsy was beautiful still and she had a good soul, but she believed in all these things that were not true and would say these things about herself that were absolutely wrong. She walked in her own thick cloud of negative energy that she generated herself, but she could not see this. She could not see herself. She was blind.

That's the problem, Betsy said. I just thought that if my intention was right, if I was clear, right down the middle . . . Now I don't know what to think. Where to put it.

* * *

You might get good news tomorrow. What's on the schedule, anyway?

CAT scan, PET scan, puppy dog scan—I forget. Some kind of imaging.

Might be nothing.

Might be, Betsy said. They caught something up in Bigfork. I don't even know what to think, Robert. I don't know what to do.

She looked him squarely in the face as if she might find an answer there. RL found himself almost blushing. He could not solve this. He could not talk her down from here. Yet he wanted to save her.

I'm sorry, she said, and gave a bitter little laugh. The worst houseguest.

You know what's weird. You walked right by my pickup truck on the way into the house and you haven't given me a single word of shit about it yet.

She laughed again, and again it was not a cheerful sound.

I'm done with the earth, she said. Somebody else can save it. Somebody who's going to be around. My kids can save the earth if they want to. Myself, I'm done. Let's just go watch television.

You hate television.

* * *

Not lately, she said. Lately it's the best thing that ever happened to me.

And so they sat, side by side on the bachelor sofa, the big plush leather cool under them but gradually warming to their skin, and RL handed her the remote and got cold beer for both of them and the rain fell outside the windows as she flipped through sports, through models and model railroads and troubled faces, explosions in the sky and pictures of the very beer they were drinking, cars and chases, guns going off, earnest conversation about the flag, baseball, fighter jets shooting through the sky and always shopping shopping shopping, glossy pictures of more. She couldn't settle on anything. RL thought she wanted all of it, the whole fake world, 120 channels of nothing and all of it inside her, a world without her, a world without end. Next to her and a thousand miles away. He had never felt this lonely. He wanted to make her happy. He wanted to make her safe. He wanted whatever he wanted, and he was going to get whatever he got.

*

Only the one girl, Daniel said, and only twice. It was a drunk thing, that was all. It was really more like an accident than anything else. The fact that he was telling her was proof that she could trust him.

Layla was down in the Angler keeping Edgar company, a slow Tuesday. The rain had stopped but the water was high and dirty still and nobody much came in. She was either going to Seattle in a couple of days or she was not. There was nobody to talk to, nobody to tell. She had made her bed and now she would have to lie in it.

Hold still, Edgar said. Just like that.

The lights were on in the store part, but there were no customers this late in the afternoon. They were in the office part with the lights turned off and Edgar was making a sketch of her face. Lucky thing it was his left arm in the cast so he could still draw. Layla couldn't see the light on her own face, of course, but she could see it on his and it was pretty light, soft and gray. Anybody would look good in a light like that, soft through clouds, big unlit windows.

Tell me something, Layla said.

Anything.

Oh, never mind.

What's going on? he said. You look like you're going to cry.

Nothing, she said. Everything is one hundred percent fine.

Glad to hear it, Edgar said. He went on sketching. Sometimes Layla imagined herself in a larger life, a Russian life, a life that glittered and sparkled. In Seattle she was often reminded that she was just a girl from Montana, a hick from the sticks. She knew how to drink and she knew how to fish, but everybody else knew everything. Other times, she thought that Edgar might be discovered—he really was that good—and then he would be a famous painter and there would be pictures of her! Some connection to the glittery sparkly world. A rock band had already used one of Edgar's paintings on the cover of its CD, though the band never went anywhere. An elemental sadness inside her that she thought champagne might cure. The wind shifted and fat raindrops spattered across the glass. Do this, do that, stand that way, stand still. A kind of furtive pleasure in being told what to do. Since the accident Edgar seemed half angry all the time, the cast constantly in his way. He was home too much and the rest of the time in the shop and not out on the water, which he loved. RL loved the water, too, but not the clients so much. Edgar didn't seem to mind the clients. Something animal and likable. Layla had seen the muscles of his back as he pulled at the oars, the way a body needs to be worked. He was easy on the water, easy at the oars, his long arms elegant. The boat moved without effort, it seemed without intention, when he was on the water. But now, cooped up, there was something fussy about him, something gangly and tense. He frowned at the sketchbook, tried to fix something with the heel of his hand, but gave up then and turned the page.

Can I see?

No, he said.

Because it sucks, is why, he said, before Layla could even ask.

She went over behind him and turned the page herself. It was her face but not her face—somebody who knew more than she did, who had seen more sadness. Layla felt herself turning into that person, which was not what she wanted. All that world out there waiting for her. Times she felt like she could outrun it, if she was only fast enough, but she understood now that she would never be fast enough.

I look old, she said.

You're just tired.

She almost told him, then—Daniel the fucker. His face came to her in a rush of fresh sorrow, a sticky deep-blue liquid. Nobody loved her.

64

* * *

I am old today, she said.

Are you OK?

No, she said. Yeah. I'm all right. I'm just tired is all. You're right.

I'm going to make a cup of tea, Edgar said. Would you like a cup of tea?

No, she said. No, yeah. I'd like a cup, thanks.

The kettle was on the far side of the empty store and he left her there in that delicate light. She listened to all the small sounds, the rain on the window glass, the buzz of the neon lights, the swish of tires on wet pavement and the splash of the downspouts. After a minute, the water in the kettle getting ready to boil. Come back, come back, she thought. She wanted Edgar there again, anybody to tell her where to put her hands, how to hold her face, anybody to tell her what to do.

*

He had slept with Betsy before, a long time before. It wasn't a secret, it wasn't a key. But it wasn't anything RL liked to think about much. Like a lot of his life at the time, this experience just seemed painful and inconclusive, painful because it was inconclusive.

He remembered the shape of her body, naked, the slippery seal length of her in that hot springs in Idaho, out in the woods in the snow, snowflakes landing on their knees and hair while they watched them, stoned. Was that the time they saw the moose? Once they were lying naked in the gravel pool when a cow moose and two calves drifted into the far end of the clearing, quietly appearing out of the cedar trees and ferns and fog, and stood there grazing for an hour, paying them no mind. Once they had strange submerged sex in the water and then she rolled him out into the snow and then followed and they rolled around in the snow like seal pups, tickling and teasing. Did that even happen? It seems like another life, somebody else's.

This was a time between Dawn and Dawn, a moment when they were broken up or she was interested in somebody else or moved to California for the winter or something. She really was a terrible girlfriend. He knew exactly what he was getting into when he married her.

So: a few months, a winter through a long cold spring, a strange mix of virtue and vice, herb tea and cigarettes, brown rice and cocaine. RL used to love the hippie girls—yes, he did—before they all turned thirty and became strict and sour. Back when everybody smoked. It was a different world, looking back. He was never one of them, he kept on eating meat and drinking brown liquor and rising out of their paisley-and-perfume beds at five to drive over to Wolf Creek and fish the Missouri.

The world had seemed like a more interesting and various place then. RL wondered if it really was, or if it only seemed that way because it was all so new to him.

But they needed something from him, and he wanted something from them. Not just attention, not just sex. What? He never really knew.

That one time he woke up in a girl's bed and he could swear he'd never seen her before, left her sleeping, never saw her again . . . It was a different time. Everything felt different.

The thing with Betsy was two things: first, she stuck around— not here but with her horrible hippie husband up in the Swan but in and out of town enough to be a part of things, to turn into the person that was inside her, waiting to come out. She was still here. They were all still here.

The other thing was the way it ended. It wasn't supposed to be a lifelong deal, a marriage. They liked each other, they slept together. He brought her smoked whitefish; he brought her red wine; he took her up to the top of Snowbowl in his '65 three-quarter-ton GMC pickup and then up the ski lift itself to watch the solar eclipse. All that long spring, while the rotten snow melted outside and then froze again every evening, they drank herbal tea and whiskey and pored over maps of the Bob Marshall and the Scapegoat Wilderness, making plans about where they would go in August, up on Scapegoat Mountain and then over to the Chinese Wall, or maybe over to the White River, which was supposed to be full of big fat cutthroat, dumb as nails. In March they went to Seattle, to drink coffee and visit some friends of hers. In April they drove to Utah for the desert sun.

It was good, he thought. They were partners, traveling companions. But then she went off tree planting when the snow cleared out of the back country that spring, a crew from Oregon, working out of Avery, Idaho. She used to ride the locomotives back and forth to the bars of Missoula, weekends when they got paid and at first the other weekends, too. She would come to see him. The Milwaukee was going out of business, nobody cared anymore and they knew this good-looking lesbian girl, Denise, who was an honest-to-God brakeman on the line. A couple of times RL went to visit her by rail—it was hours less time than driving, sitting up in the lead locomotive as they crawled across the Bitterroot Divide, miles of green nothing and granite in front of them, the wilderness closing behind.

* * *

And then that was it. Over. One payday weekend in July, he waited for her all Friday night and not a peep. Nothing all weekend or the week after that or after that.

He heard from friends through other friends that she was all right, just not coming into town—something was going on, nobody knew exactly what. Just gone. Left him with his candles ready to light and a bottle of gin in the freezer. That summer was the first one he worked for Saul Pohler and that old bastard kept him busier than shit ferrying trailers and packing lunches and tying flies and even guiding a couple of times when things got desperate—though Saul didn't think he knew enough to guide, told him so—and the summer passed and then, in September, came Betsy's wedding invitation. Elizabeth Ann Broughton. He never knew her middle name till then.

*

The last clear hot day of summer they took off from the state park at Big Arm in Howard's speedboat and headed out toward Wild Horse Island, June, Howard and Layla. It was just after Labor Day, and the big fancy lake houses that lined the shores like railway stations built for fun were all deserted except for one or two: an older couple reading in the sun, a college girl tanning on the end of her dock, lizardly.

The lake stretched twenty miles north from here, blue as an eye, ending in the white Swan Range. Last week's rain had fallen as snow in the mountains. It felt like summer down on the lake—it *was* summer—but up in the mountains the seasons were turning. It was a Tuesday and a very pleasant sense of playing hooky for all of them, a stolen day while the rest of the world was at work. In fact, Howard was working—a cabin he needed to take a look at out on the island—

and neither of the women had anywhere in particular to be. June had rotated through her normal weekend shift and UW didn't start for another two weeks.

June had nowhere else to be, but still that delicious taste of a stolen day. Howard had traded his Western hat for a baseball cap that said King Ropes Sheridan Wyoming; he stood behind the wheel in bare feet, cleaving the breeze with the prow of his mustache, going much faster than was necessary. The cool lake water whipped into spray and misted the women where they sat in the stern, lounging with Diet Cokes. So many gifts, June thought: this day, this sunlight. Days when living felt easy. She didn't get too many of them, but she knew—when they pushed off from the dock with a full tank of gas and a loaded cooler, nowhere to go on purpose and her cell phone locked safely in her car—that this would be an easy day.

Even Layla, Layla was a gift. Without Layla, it would have just been June and Howard, and she wasn't ready for that yet. If she was ever going to be ready for that. That mysterious third party, she thought. Yesterday she had said she would come along and then felt, all day, a hot little ball of dread in her belly. A half-dozen times she had picked up the phone to tell him she couldn't come after all but she couldn't think of the right lie. She was no good at lying, anyway. Then Layla had come by, without warning or explanation. She said she was out for a drive and saw her light on. June thought this sounded unlikely. Her house was eleven miles out of town and on the opposite side of the valley. But whatever she came for, June would never know. She was glad to see her. They drank a glass of wine on the porch and listened to the quiet night, talking about nothing. Maybe that was it, June thought. Maybe all the girl needed was another heart beating next to hers, a little breath and conversation.

* * *

At the end of the night, without asking Howard first, she invited Layla to the lake.

Howard seemed surprised but not upset to find this out. She couldn't read him worth a damn.

That mysterious third party, June thought. Someone to perform for, someone to referee. The grind of small mistake on small mistake. It was so hard to know what to say! Like coming in halfway through a movie, she thought, trying to figure out what came before. Howard had brought wine coolers and hard lemonade for them but nonalcoholic beer for himself, which meant—what? June realized at the sight of the O'Doul's that she had never seen Howard take a drink, yet she was sure or almost sure (why?) that he had had a drink or two along the way. But having Layla on board meant that the question couldn't be raised or even noticed; it was all smooth sailing and small talk and easy.

Howard suddenly cut the engine to trolling speed and the front of the boat lurched down into the water. He stopped in front of a soaring glass-fronted house on the shore, pointed toward the sky like praying hands.

See that place?

The women nodded.

Coach of the Detroit Pistons, Howard said. Never seen a single person there.

Let's go burn it down, said Layla.

* * *

Yes, let's, said June.

Howard kicked the boat up to planing speed again. None of that, he shouted. We're in favor of real estate on this boat.

June said nothing but she wasn't so sure—all these millions of dollars, all these empty, quiet houses. The only places that seemed occupied were the old mom-and-pop operations, little leftover cabins with canoes on the lawn, but these were dwarfed and outnumbered by the new money places, soaring glass and big speedboats up on covered shore stations. A quick fierce nostalgia lying there in the sun—her and Taylor and sometimes RL and Dawn would rent a place for a week in the summer, smoking pot on the dock and watching the shooting stars. . . . It seemed like minutes ago; it seemed impossible that the baby girl Dawn had brought bundled to June's wedding was across from her now, long legged and pretty. Taylor, she thought, shooting across the water in another man's boat. Taylor. Even the world they lived in was gone, the little rat shacks and falling-down cottages with names like "Our Back Achers."

She shouldn't be here. She knew it suddenly but completely. A betrayal.

Then pulled herself back in. A trap, a comfort, a sameness in that sadness. It was not her friend, she reminded herself. Don't make a friend of your disease.

She looked up to find Layla grinning at her.

You looked like you were having an argument with yourself, she said.

* * *

I was, said June, and grinned right back.

You want to go swimming?

You think it's warm enough?

I am, Layla said. And that water's not going to change much.
Captain Howard!

Yes, ma'am.

See if you can find us a swimming spot.

Howard shut the engine off then and there, and the boat eased
back down into its own wake, white frothy water surging past them.
He said, As good a spot as any.

A little yang, June thought. An excess of masculine energy.
Then before she could think about it and stop herself, she stood and
stripped her T-shirt off in one motion and dove.

The water was instant cold, enveloping. As soon as her fingers
touched the cold water, her body screamed *mistake* and tried to lev-
itate but could not stop itself and plunged deep into the even colder
depths. Somewhere she heard another splash and knew it must be
Layla diving after her. June swam to the surface and shook the water
out of her eyes, and there was Layla and they both started to shriek
from the cold. Like little kids in a public pool they screamed and
shrieked again, loud and high-pitched and piercing, pure yin.

They shrieked to please themselves and they did. When June
looked up, though, she saw Howard Emerson looking down from

the stern like a stern judge, a hanging judge thought June, and turned to Layla and screamed again, louder. Layla screamed back. They paid no attention to Howard. I love this girl, thought June.

Then a cannonball splash and Howard was in the water with them, or mostly in the water; his cap set firmly on his head and his mustache dry and bushy. He had taken his tiny sunglasses off at least. He blinked at them from blank face to blank face (June had tried his glasses on once in secret and his eyes really were that close to useless) and for once looked powerless, confused. June liked him then. Stripped of his manly shell, that chitinous outer layer, he looked momentarily approachable. He could be like that always. He could be lovable.

This reminds me of New Zealand, he said, and the bubble burst. He was right again. He was right always.

But why was June such a fussbudget? She didn't need to be.

Like porcupines, she thought. Very, very carefully.

When were you in New Zealand? she asked brightly.

A while back, he said. A few decades ago. Back when it was still a long way off the beaten trail.

And what were you doing there?

Ah, he said, letting his legs float up in front of him, paddling idly with his hands to stay afloat. He said, I had this other life. I was kind of a surf bum.

* * *

Well, that sounds interesting, she said; though really all this dressing up, these other lives made her nervous. Cowpoke, surfer, Indian chief, she thought. It was like dating the Village People.

The blue water and the mountains rising right up out of it, Howard said. Snow on the mountains. Of course, it was completely different there but it looked quite similarly.

Similar, she thought. Not *similarly*. But she didn't say anything.

This water is *cold*, she said.

You get used to it.

If you don't freeze and die first.

Nobody's going to die, said Howard. You can't die from this. If it was a little colder, maybe. I fell out of a boat once and into Puget Sound, and it was a close shave whether they could get the boat turned around in time.

Was this a little boat?

No, it was quite a good size, thirty feet or more.

How do you fall out of a boat?

There's nothing to it, really.

The thing not said, she thought. It had to be drinking. Fighting. Something he didn't want to talk about yet, some chapter closed and hopefully long gone. She lay back in the water and looked up at the deep blue sky, scatters and rags of high cloud. The top six or eight inches of water were nearly warm from the sun. What did she want from him?

That was a difficult time in my life, he said. Seattle was.

Just hearing him say this made June realize that she didn't know where Layla was. He would never say a thing like this within her earshot. She looked around and didn't see her anywhere.

Where'd she go? June said.

The girl?

The girl, June said. Where'd she go?

Howard whipped himself upright and scanned the horizon with his blurry eyes. June wheeled around in watery panic herself and then, by accident, saw Layla's seal head surface a hundred feet away, swimming for China. Slippery porpoise, she thought. Pretty girl.

She's there, June said.

Where?

Way over there, June said, and pointed, and Howard pointed his head in that direction, though he would never see her. June was touched by this, his willingness to protect. Manly men and difficult girls, she thought. Where the hell was Layla going?

And why was everybody going crazy all at once? Couldn't Layla just wait her turn?

* * *

Layla! she cried. Layla, where are you going?

But her voice was lost immediately in the vastness of the water, dying out in a few feet. June felt small and the water felt cold.

We'd better go get her, June said.

I still don't see her, Howard said.

Well, she's out there, June said. We'd better go get her.

What's she doing?

Going cuckoo, June said. I don't know.

They clambered aboard via the swim ladder and there ensued a brief moment of truth: Howard's considerable-looking dingus under his wet bathing suit, June's fat and sag under his gaze. Oh, the body, June thought. He was small without his clothes and white as a Scotsman where the sun didn't strike him, on his upper arms and back and belly and legs, but he had a firm look and he was not at all fat. June knew that she looked all right for who she was. But she had seen herself too often in the mirrors of the gym to like being looked at. She was good for her age but it was not a good age.

Howard was a gentleman, though, tucked his eyes away and pulled a T-shirt on and fired up the boat and chased off after Layla, who he could see now, with his little sunglasses on.

What is that girl up to? he said, more to himself than to June.

* * *

She didn't have an answer. Briefly considered pulling a shirt on over her wet suit but that felt like a coward's way. This is me, she thought, a little shopworn, a little used. This is me.

They caught up to Layla, and Howard cut the engine.

June asked, What are you doing?

Layla dog-paddled for a moment and then said, Swimming. I felt like swimming.

I could see that. Do you want to come aboard?

I don't think so. Is that all right?

June looked at Howard, asking. He said, We've got all day.

All right then, Layla said, and dove under the water and came up into the crawl, a long-limbed easy movement without hurry or splash, and started for—where? She was pointed at Bigfork, a dozen miles away. She headed for the big empty middle of the lake, out of sight of houses, only the hills and mountains and water. After a few minutes Howard fired the boat up again and they followed her at trolling speed, staying well back, letting Layla alone as she swam into the empty heart of the lake. The quiet, when they shut the boat off again, was immediate, enveloping. It was a Tuesday, and everybody else was at work, and the three of them were alone on the lake.

*

Rainy late September, four o'clock, everybody in a hurry and nobody getting anywhere, brake lights reflected in the glossy streets, RL driving the big Ford pickup and Betsy next to him on the bench seat with her baskets and bundles.

I am shit scared, Betsy said.

I understand, RL said.

No, you don't.

No, he said. I don't.

After a minute she said, I think they just want me in there tonight to keep an eye on me. Nothing's even going to happen till tomorrow morning. I think they just want to make sure I don't eat anything.

After a minute more she said, I think they just want to make sure I'm not enjoying myself.

You want to get a beer? We've got time, I think. Glass of wine?

I don't want to be late.

Late for what? You said it yourself.

Oh, she said. Oh, OK. Just someplace without smoking.

Because smoking is bad for you.

That business will kill you, Betsy said.

You can't smoke anyplace anymore, RL said. Those days are over. You don't get out much, do you?

I don't want to, Robert. If it was up to me, I'd just crawl back into my little hole, you know, lead my little life till it was over. I like my own bed and my own cooking.

Sitting across from him at a table next to the window of the Depot Bar, the rain light washing over her face and a tall brown glass of ale on the table in front of her, Betsy said, You can still smoke in Liquid Louie's.

I'd forgotten about Liquid Louie's, RL said. El dumpo magnifico. Does that insane bitch still tend bar there?

* * *

Carol-Ann? She's my neighbor.

I don't care if she's the pope, said RL. Threw me out of there one night in the middle of a snowstorm. I said something bad about the Green Bay Packers.

She does love the Packers, Betsy said. Then they both fell silent. It was early, the hour before happy hour, and they had the place to themselves, almost, and the soft gray daylight filtering through the glass made her face look pretty and soft, almost young. RL could remember the shape of her body, long and tall, her vivid giddy sudden smile, like a break in the clouds on a windy day, the sunlight racing through. . . . It was a mistake, he guessed, if you had to decide one way or the other. Back then, it didn't seem like you had to decide, right or wrong, it was just something that happened. An experience, at a time when he was hungry for experience, when they all were. Where did it come from, RL wondered, this wish to make each day identical to the one before? He made his coffee the same way every morning, read the paper back to front, wore the same brand of blue jeans for the last twenty years at least. The pre-death, maybe, RL thought.

Betsy looked at him and smiled. She knew what he was thinking, exactly. It went without saying.

Did I tell you about the water festival? she asked.

If you did, I don't remember.

Right when I got out of college, she said. The first time I went traveling anywhere by myself, I went to Thailand. Before I met you.

Susan Cohen was supposed to come with me but she got mono, or she said she did. Really, I think she just got into her boyfriend and didn't want to come. Anyway, I either had to not go or go by myself, which I really didn't want to. Is this boring?

No.

All this old-time stuff. It just seems like a long time ago. Like another life almost.

But you did go.

I did, she said. I didn't want to but I had a passport and a ticket and I just thought, Fuck it, I can come home early if I need to. It was a weird time, too, because my parents had just died. I had all this money, but it was all the money I was ever going to have. I never knew what to feel.

I remember, RL said—and he did, remembered holding her as she wept. He drove her to the airport for the trip home, for the funeral, but the plane was iced down in Spokane and hours late. They wound up tearful drunk in the airport bar, watching the occasional small flakes of snow drift down through the white ice fog. Even at the time, he thought it was strange that she didn't have anyone closer, some girl to drive her to the airport and hold her hand. He didn't mind doing it—he liked it, it made him feel useful—but their moment had come and gone a year or more before and now he was just a friend, with a sad drunk girl in an airport.

I went down to Phuket first, Betsy said. Sex and drugs and rock and roll, party time all the time. I hated it. You know me—I'm such a sourpuss! But I did love the ocean, the feel of the water and the blue sky and the clouds. And the sand was just so soft and white. I ended up on an island south of there, back before, when it was almost all Thai people. I rented this little, really awful concrete bungalow and there was a bookstore on Phuket and all I did was read and lie in the sun, even through the hot parts of the day. I can still remember it when I close my eyes, the feel of the sun and the sand under me. Part of it was about being in my body and just feeling it, and part of it was about not wanting to exist, you know, just obliterating myself. Erasing. I'd go down to the bars at night and drink Scotch whiskey. Then sit in the sun and read *Anna Karenina*. Little lizards all around. That's where all this came from.

All this what?

The melanoma. From the sun on Phi Phi Don. Even then I knew it wasn't good for me but it was, it felt good. Just to burn something out of me.

You believe that?

Yes, I do. I believe in intention. I wanted to erase myself and look: it's working.

She grinned at him and sipped her beer. A cold creepy feeling along his spine. She really had no hope at all. Again he felt the Galahad urge to save her, to fetch her back into the world, among the living. He knew he couldn't, knew he might have to try.

Betsy said, I met a Thai boy, my age. He was the only one drunker than I was. Everybody else was smoking Thai pot back then and I wish I had some now but then we both just liked to get messed up on Scotch. So we just woke up hungover one morning and decided we had to get out of there, I thought we were just killing ourselves and Ray thought we needed to find a spiritual place. You know, he was a really nice person, Ray was. He could have done anything with me. Nobody was keeping track, and I was just giving myself away to anybody who wanted it. Fucked-up things happened all the time there.

She stopped, remembering. Then said, A girl ended up, they found her chained to a bed. Canadian girl. But, no, Ray got us on a bus and found some Coca-Cola and aspirin with codeine for the hangovers and we drove all the way two days north to Chang Mai. I was like, shaking the whole time.

Ray? RL asked.

His real name was about a block long, Betsy said. Everybody just called him Ray. He knew people everywhere. We got to Chang Mai and right away, he had us staying with his cousin in this, like, I don't know, a garage or something behind his house. I had money, we could have stayed in a hotel, except this seemed like more of an adventure. Also, I don't know, maybe there weren't any hotels. People came from everywhere for the water festival. There were elephants in the streets. Just the clothes and colors and everybody smiling and the little kids—you know, they were the first ones who started off throwing water at each other and then it was just water everywhere. I was so stupid, I was wearing a white T-shirt and after five minutes it was like, what do *you* think of my bra? but nobody cared. I don't even know if they noticed.

You look pretty.

What?

Just talking about it, it makes you happy, makes you pretty, RL said.

Well, I was, she said. I was happy. I was *cool*, Robert. Once in a lifetime, I was in the right place at the right time. But just, I don't know, being in the crowd with everybody laughing and singing and water everywhere, it was like for just one moment I just kind of dissolved, just an atom with a bunch of other atoms, you know? Instead of *my* problems and my little life, it was like being part of something bigger, like a cell in a body—I don't know how to explain it. It was beautiful. It was really beautiful.

It sounds like it.

But I wonder, now, if I let something into my life that I shouldn't have. Some little pill that took this long to dissolve.

You didn't.

You don't know.

No, RL said. I don't.

*

Then came the glory days of fall. The larch turned
gold in the high country, gold on green, and the cottonwood leaves
drifted down the river in all their colors. Edgar couldn't stand it
anymore, went up to Rock Creek with his cast wrapped in plastic
and fished one-handed into a brilliant afternoon, wading from the
bank into the cold clean river. He was fine with the fishing part
except that when he caught a fish it was a clusterfuck completely,
and there was a moth hatch going on and a fish lying hungry and
heedless in every bank. He took a fifteen-inch rainbow from under
a willow tree and lost the fly and tippet trying to release it. The fly
would work its way out of the rainbow's lip in a few days but still it
bothered him. Not the fly—a nickel's worth of feathers and the five
minutes of work that went into it—but the fish wearing it, the extra
bit of junk on the streambed, for the few months before it rusted to

nothing. . . . It wasn't anything, really, anything of consequence, but it bothered him. A fish wearing a yellow stimulator.

He caught another little brown and this time lost his sunglasses in the water, trying to unhook him. This was not going to work.

He set the handle of the rod in his teeth and this time managed—with the forceps in his broken hand—to release the little brown and then felt around underwater for his glasses until his arm went numb from the cold. He couldn't move his feet so as not to break the glasses. When he could move his fingers again, he put the rod back in his mouth and raised the cast above him and felt the bottom again. This time he found them. The glasses seemed to be fine, unscratched, But his fishing day was over.

A burst of baby rage. It wasn't fair. He had so nothing to himself, with the child and the job, so few hours to call his own and he had driven all this way . . . and then the anger was gone. He still had the afternoon and no one expecting him till suppertime.

Edgar sat down at the edge of the gravel bank and watched the stream go by. He lit a cigarette from the illicit pack he had bought in Clinton. On the way home, he would toss whatever was left of the pack and buy some mints and hope that Amy didn't smell it on him under the smell of sunblock, sweat and river water. The water in front of him tailed out of a riffle, a little way upstream, into a broad and deceptively deep pool at the base of a cliff. Something Japanese and pretty about the dark circling water under the rock wall. The moths, little white ones, were landing in the water out of the evergreen trees upstream and the tongue of the tailout was carrying them down the dead middle of the river, where dozens of fat trout lay in wait for them. Easy pickings for a two-armed man.

Did Amy really not know? She must smell the smoke on him. Was she just pretending not to? It didn't seem like her at all, and yet . . . This whole business of marriage felt baffling to him, a game without rules, especially since the baby had come along. Edgar loved the baby, loved the afternoons when it was just the two of them, loved the smell of the baby's head and her tiny, blunt hands. But things between them were different with the baby around.

Insoluble, he thought. Then wished he had brought pad and paper with him. Then he was glad he had not. Edgar did not often get to enjoy the luxury of idleness. He didn't approve of idleness, or like it, but it was good for him sometimes to stop all the usual doing and going and just look at what was in front of his eyes. The sky was a high clear blue that shimmered blue on the water. Edgar looked at the line where the shadow of the cliff met the sunlight on the water, the way the rock reflected black, deep brown and gray next to the sky blue. Downstream the river opened up into a wider valley, an old homestead, the cabin and barns long abandoned and tumbledown. In the near bend stood the overgrown remains of an orchard, the trees half dead and untended but the branches weighted down with apples still. Edgar wondered if the apples were any good. He was half in love with these old trees, their perseverance.

In a minute he'd go over to the orchard and pick one of those apples. As soon as he was done with this cigarette.

He lay back in the soft green grass and looked up into the clear sky. The way the color was so light, almost washed-out and intense at the same time. The things he didn't understand about light.

* * *

This unexpected empty time. It was like putting your foot down in the dark and finding no stair there, the tangible lack of presence.

She came through the sunlight and the tall grass, a translucent cloud of dry pollen before her and around her, tall and quick, confident in the step. A white skirt swinging around her long legs. Why did he know her? Dark hair tied back. It felt like he had been expecting her all along, like this was what he had been waiting for without knowing it. Then she came closer, and stopped a couple of feet away, facing him, long-limbed, serious. He felt—what? He didn't know what he felt. Excitement, fear.

I saw your truck, Layla said.

What were you doing up here?

I just got restless, I wanted to go for a drive.

It's a long drive.

I was really restless, she said.

She turned her back on him then, went down to the edge of the water, a few feet away. She wore a green blouse with no sleeves and he admired the length of her, the color of her skin, the tiny downy hairs on her arms that shone in the sunlight. Her feet in sandals were slim and pretty on the river rocks.

They're rising out of there like motherfuckers, she said. How come you're not fishing?

* * *

He raised the cast for her to see, wrapped in a plastic whole-wheat-bread bag.

I tried, he said.

They were deep in the wilderness, forty miles in either direction to a gas pump. They were almost alone except for the few other cars and pickups in the turnouts along the road, and these were fishermen who wanted to be alone themselves, alone with the water. Past the old orchard, the valley opened up, and he could see the hillside above, green forest giving way to rock to sky. Bighorn sheep lived up in those rocks. Something clarifying and clean about the way the sky drew your eye up, lifted you out of yourself.

When he looked back down again, she was still there.

I could hook 'em fine, he said. I just couldn't land them.

I haven't been up here since last spring, she said. I don't know why. It's the prettiest place.

I haven't either. Now it's almost closing time.

I go back to Seattle tomorrow.

Then they were kissing. Then after some small comedy, fumbling with the pants and fishing apparatus, then they were naked in the tall green grass with the last sun of the year falling down on them, the touch of her, the length of her, the inevitability. This was written somewhere, it felt to Edgar. This was always going to happen. And then it did.

*

You're here awfully early in the morning, Betsy said. I didn't know you were such an early riser.

RL looked at the clock on the wall of the hospital room. It was six thirty in the evening.

I need to tell my mother, she said.

The thing about it was her eyes, he thought. Her eyes were clear and lucid and it seemed like she was right there in the room with you. Then she opened her mouth and there was no telling what would come out. Her mother had been dead since college.

Then the pain hit again and she disappeared inside. Maybe it wasn't pain, maybe it was confusion, illness, something. Her eyes went blank but they stayed open and her mouth opened a little and she breathed hard through her mouth like she was walking uphill and her forehead and cheeks broke out in a cold sweat. Her skin went pink and gray in these moments of pain and sometimes he could see fear in her eyes. Ashes and roses, animal flight. I wouldn't make a dog do this, he thought. I'd put a dog down, before I made him go through this.

Then she was asleep, or something like it. Gone, anyway, the light out of her eyes and her eyes half closed. It was spooky to look at them. All he could see were the whites. The room was half dark, somewhere in the windowless internals of the hospital, and the lights of the various instruments and pumps and gauges shone like a distant city on a hill. The oxygen breathed with her and the drug pump rattled, clicked and cycled. She might come back around but she probably wouldn't soon, at least that was how it had been lately.

On the edge of organ failure, is what the oncologist said. There were other possibilities. An ordinary infection, a case of the flu could speed her away.

RL didn't know what he was doing there. It wouldn't make any difference to Betsy, she didn't know what planet she was on. Plus she had a husband and all. This felt at times that it was really not his job, not his place, not his cross to bear. But then, when he was at home and she was here, he felt this constant pull. She shouldn't suffer this alone.

RL sat in a pastel chair next to the bed, a pile of magazines next to him: *Travel & Leisure, Field & Stream, Modern Maturity*, the dregs of the waiting room pile. He had read everything twice. Maybe, he thought, maybe it was as simple as this: he wouldn't wish himself to go through this alone. Everybody dies alone, everybody said so, but this was—what?—a lyric from a rock song or something. Everybody smokes in Hell. So what? Among the living we love company. He liked to think that she would know, but even if she didn't, it was the right thing to do. Besides, Layla was back in Seattle and without her, RL's house was empty and creepy. It was always like that when she left.

Ann child, said Betsy. What are you doing, baby?

Her daughter, eleven years old. RL had never met her. Betsy settled back into the pillow. RL felt a momentary threat of tears, sentimental . . .

She had her reasons for not wanting them around, Betsy did. There was some small chance—7 percent said one doctor, 12 percent said another—that she would live, and she did not want her children to see her in this extreme. It was true, this part; she looked like the she-devil in a Japanese movie, come to tempt the sailors into Hell. Even her tear ducts looked red and torn. Her hair was tangled and she smelled of her own vomit. He would not want Layla to see him so.

And yet . . . He did not think that Layla would stay away. She wouldn't care what he wanted. She would come anyway. This was the mystery part: where was her husband, Roy? Taking care of the children, was the party line. Feeding the chickens, the children, the thousand small chores of a country place. RL did not believe this, but he did not know what else to believe. They tended toward the practical and stern, Betsy and Roy. They were rough people, country hippies. There was a right and a wrong and if this was right, they would find a way to do right because that was the kind of people they were.

Pizza, said the lady with the alligator purse.

RL went out into the hallway. Wayne, the nurse's aide, was joking at the main station down the hall. The new duty nurse, whose name RL did not yet know, was looking at him with spaniel attention, waiting for the punch line. An empty gurney with wrinkled sheets, a pillow with an outline of a human head, waited outside one of the rooms, some new emergency. They lived with emergency every day here, with death, dismemberment, bad smells and weeping wives. RL did not grudge them their jokes and brightly colored uniforms, the fresh flowers on the ledge of the nurse's station, but he could not share these small comforts with them.

Fading daylight filled the hallway outside. RL was surprised to find it so. Inside, in the rooms where all the dirty work took place, it was always night. Where was Roy? This autumn twilight, lonely time. The only time he missed the city, men in black jackets, women in makeup and dresses, hurrying to meet each other in the falling day. All those other people he could have been. All those hundreds of doors closing, one by one, until there was just the one door left, the last one. A friendly bartender, a cool drink, a meeting, a woman. I am lonely, RL thought. I am lonely. I was born lonely. I am best so.

*

What made June angry was people who went through the fields behind her house, down to the river, and never shut the gates again so the neighbor cows would end up all over her pasture. Also, these same people when they stole the last few tomatoes out of her garden when she was at work. Also Howard, when he never answered his cell phone when she knew perfectly well that he had caller ID and knew it was her and June wasn't a time-waster, was she? No. Direct and to the point. She wouldn't call if she didn't need to talk to him.

The people she got stuck behind who were trying to make a left onto Reserve Street which was impossible and took forever, these people infuriated her.

* * *

Out-of-state checks, welfare payments, Argentinean banks—
there was no telling what kind of mayhem she could cause in a
checkout line just because she was in it. Women who watched the
checker ring up $105 in groceries and only when the last item was
tallied did they begin to search for their checkbooks in their bot-
tomless handbags. Those same women in the drive-up teller lane,
filling out their endless deposit slips, doing the math wrong.

What completely pissed June off was the hospice, the way they
never paid the aides and janitors enough to live on so it was always
somebody new, always a fresh sad story. Last month it was a dude
named Mad Dog, at least that was the name he had tattooed across
the back of his neck in plain sight. Mad Dog was a cheerful or
maybe overcheerful janitor and a comfort to the dying, but then he
went out one weekend and came back on Monday with all his teeth
kicked in. A few days after that he just stopped showing up. Seri-
ously, June did not need that kind of energy in her life. She could
barely care enough about her own people. Also, obviously, foreign
policy, the whole Iraq mess, the fight-picking with Iran.

The whole oil business made her so mad, she went out and
traded her little pickup for a Prius one Saturday. Now the Prius
smelled like horse manure because she had no other way to get it for
her garden. Also people mistook her for a hippie vegetarian Birken-
stocker. OK, she did have Birkenstocks. Why did people have to
judge her for it? It irritated her, this constant rush to judgment.

Do not even get June started on the bishops, the ones who
closed their eyes all those years while the priests were molesting little boys, the bastards in their brocade robes who tried to cover it up
and now all the money was going to the lawyers instead of the poor.

* * *

The Republicans. All of them, even the nice ones.

The pro-lifers, the ones outside the Blue Mountain Clinic with their pictures of fetuses.

The living. She couldn't stand the living anymore. So headstrong, set in their ways, blind to possibility. The dying, she loved. Some old cowboy down from Arlee, been spitting and falling off horses and driving pickup trucks for seventy years and now here he is between clean sheets, talking about his emotions, listening to Arvo Pärt, music that sounds like angels, tears rolling down his cheeks, cheeks worn to the color of wood from seventy years in the wind and the rain. The vulnerability, possibility, the opening up. June loved this. It was like nothing could change until it was too late, but then at the last minute anything was possible. She felt them, looking over the fence at whatever would come next and seeing how small the operation was, how little it mattered, and then they could just let go and love.

The living, on the other hand. June just couldn't stand the living.

*

Oh, she thought. OK, the ship . . .

She woke, four thirty by the bedside clock, cobwebbed in dreams. The ship was leaving and they would all be left behind if she could not get RL, June, Daniel and her old dog Martha onto the gangplank in time, but one of them was always getting lost and the others would not stay put when she went to look for the stray. *Martha, my love,* she thought, and almost cried. An ancient Australian shepherd, lame but game. Pretty girl, Layla used to call her. My little pretty girl.

Layla was sitting by the window, looking out at the sleeping street, when Daniel came in shorts and a T-shirt to join her.

What's up?

* * *

Nothing.

Come to bed.

In a minute.

What's wrong?

Nothing.

What do you mean, nothing?

What I said, she said. Nothing. I'm fine. Everything's fine.

Come back to bed, then.

In a minute, she said. Really, I'm fine. I'll be there in a minute.

He put his hand on her shoulder, then, but tentatively. He didn't know if he should or not. Women were a mystery to him, they had established that much. Daniel was just a willing little victim, buffeted by estrogen and perfume. Layla just wanted him to say what he wanted. But he wouldn't.

After a minute he took his hand away and then the rest of him, back to the bedroom without another word.

Outside the fallen rainwater was dripping from the monkey-puzzle trees in the park across the street. An ocean breeze was whipping the streetlight shadows around. Three thirty in the morning, the sidewalks empty. It made her cold just to look at the empty street. All she wore was a pair of his flannel boxers and a T-shirt that said *Sputnik* on the front in Russian letters. That and a pair of wool socks. She had been crying earlier and her nose was red and her eyes were pink as bunny eyes. Layla went to the thermostat and turned it up to 73 degrees, from 63, where Daniel had set it. His parents had bought him this apartment across from Volunteer Park, and he could afford the nickel it would take to heat this place to a human temperature. Also, it would annoy him, which was fine with Layla.

But *why*.

Why sleep with somebody you didn't even like? His semen drooling out of her still. Looking out at the empty sidewalk, she felt a thousand country-western songs rising up in her chest, all the ones about loneliness. All in a tangle. She wanted Daniel but she couldn't stand the way he did things, which made her wonder if what she wanted was really this boy at all but some picture in her mind. His smile. A day at the ocean, his glossy hair in the sea breeze. She felt like she had ordered him from a catalog, only to find that he was not exactly what she had wanted.

Cunt prick bastard fuckhead. His dick in someone else's mouth.

Outside a couple was walking home along the edge of the park, a punky pair in plaid and black jeans, weaving drunk, bouncing shoulders, laughing. They didn't know Layla was watching from her dark window. Everything wet, dripping, though the rain had stopped. Along the iron palings the boy stopped and leaned against the fence and looked up into the sky. The girl pressed into him, hips on hips. They were drunk, she could see it from the window, his pale hand on her breast. She said something to make him laugh and he pulled her tight against him, against the dripping fence.

* * *

Suddenly Layla was lit with desire, buzzing with it, an insect swarm around her eyes and ears and mouth, the memory of him in the grass, the best mistake, the best mistake . . . Layla was dizzy with it, the thought of him, his delicate hands. And it was all wrong and it was all a mistake, she knew it. She should not want what she could not get. None of this could end well, not with Daniel, not with Edgar. She would end up alone, unloved. It didn't matter. What was wrong with her? this emptiness inside, the place that wouldn't fill, not with any of them inside her. More and more and more and more and she always ended up with less. I want, she thought, looking down at the drunk couple. I want what you have and I want more. I want all of it. I want more of it than there is.

Come to bed, said Daniel. He was standing there in his stocking feet, like a man in a joke.

He said, It's late. Come to bed and we can talk in the morning.

Fuck you, she thought, and almost said it.

Lay there awake with Daniel breathing next to her. Obedient, she thought. Like a wife. She may have slept a little, deeper into the night, and if she did, her last expiring thought was of the limitless array of stars above them, the Milky Way stretching like a river of light, and of the clouds and buildings and walls between the stars and the bed where she lay trying to sleep. A citizen of the Milky Way, she thought. That's me.

*

The first three days after the chemo, Betsy stayed in RL's back bedroom, mainly sleeping. He brought her tea and clementines and soup, and kept fresh flowers in the room, the curtains open all day to catch the last strong light of fall. He bought her a little extra television to keep her company, and he would hear it sometimes in the night, three or four in the morning, whatever was on at that hour. She didn't really have much to say. She seemed confused, injured in the brain. She looked infinitely older than her forty-four years.

On the fourth day, it was time for her to go back up the valley. He piled her bags and baskets in the little seat behind the main seat of his pickup and then went back inside for Betsy. A damp, blustery day with a high sky and a look of wildness in the ragged clouds.

When he was younger, RL would dream himself to be an Indian on a day like this, a Lakota, looking into a long cold winter. Then he would imagine himself up for the job, which he no longer did. He would die of the cold. On the other hand, in the old days with the Lakota, he would have been dead by now anyway so maybe it didn't matter so much.

Days like this he missed his father.

Betsy looked tired was all. She seemed much like herself otherwise. She stayed quiet all through town and on the interstate, but when they turned up the Blackfoot, when they left town behind, she seemed to lift and brighten.

Did you ever think I was hard of smelling? she asked.

Like you couldn't smell as well as other people? I never gave it a minute's thought. So, I guess, no.

Me neither, Betsy said. But since this whole business came up, I can smell like a bloodhound or something. Every little thing. It's really more of a curse than a blessing.

I imagine, RL said. Especially in this truck.

I wasn't going to say anything, she said. Ha! It's actually not that bad. But, you know, it's just really strange, everybody's perfume and deodorant. I can tell a smoker from a mile off, too. It makes me wonder what-all else I've been missing. You ever think about that?

What?

* * *

How much of your brain is just shut off, she said. Too much information, I guess. Too hard to make sense of things if you have to think about everything.

RL drove for a while, thinking. Betsy was a little like a dude in the way she came up with curious conversations out of nowhere. He thought about smelling, which he couldn't remember doing before. Did he have any opinions or ideas? Of course she was not dude-shaped or dude-smelling but there was something about her.

Sometimes I think, he said, the thing we call instinct, it's just that sense of smell. Not like the thing that's at the front of your brain, you know, where it smells like peppermint or something, but way down in the monkey brain, the reptile brain. Pheromones. You meet somebody and you fall in love, boom.

I don't think I've ever been in love, she said.

RL didn't know what to say so he kept on driving, up and over the hill where Lubrecht was and down into the valley where the old Lindbergh ranch lay, now a high-end dude ranch where you could spend three thousand dollars to stay in a tent. There was so much wrong with this that RL couldn't even start to count. Fresh white snow already on the high peaks of the Bob Marshall, miles away, and RL felt his heart fly out of his chest at the sight of them and fly up into the high country, his true and secret home. He felt the presence of his shadow, that other life that was the opposite of the one he was leading, fresh and clean and out in the open.

As they passed the fiberglass bull at Clearwater Junction and headed for her home, RL said, There's different kinds of love.

* * *

You love your rivers, she said.

I do.

I love my children, she said. I don't have to tell you about that.

No, you don't.

But that thing that just comes along and knocks you down, she said. The whirlwind. I've read about it but I don't even know if I believe in it.

You used to be in love all the time, RL said. Back in college, I don't think a week went by where you weren't.

That wasn't real love.

You seemed to think it was. At the time.

I didn't know anything, she said bitterly.

I always thought it was like being hot or cold or scared of heights, RL said. If you thought you were, well, you pretty much were. It might mean something different to you now.

Listen to the expert, Betsy said, and that shut him up.

They drove in silence along the side of Placid Lake. Out in the middle sat a mansion that you could only get to by boat. A man—RL didn't remember the name—had built it and then gone broke, according to the story, and then hung himself in it. Now it sat alone and haunted in the middle of the gray lake. That was the thing, RL thought. Build your defenses strongly enough and they'll keep everybody out, but they will keep you in as well.

I'm sorry, she said after a few miles.

That's all right.

No, it isn't. I'm mean to the people who are nice to me and nice to the people who are mean to me. You should see me with the oncology staff. They're trying to save my life!

RL looked at the clock: four thirty. He was taking her back to her husband. He didn't want to. He was going to miss her, the quiet afternoons, tea and oranges. Plus, she needed saving, from this life and from this death. RL felt he was the man for the job.

Do you want to stop for a drink?

I'm not supposed to drink, she said.

That's not what I asked.

I could have a Shirley Temple or something. If you want to stop.

We can keep going if you want to.

That's all right, she said.

But when they pulled into the parking lot of the Dirty Shame, she had changed her mind again. I'm tired, she said, and all that smoke! She should just head back up the hill.

RL said, Sure! as brightly as he could to hide his disappointment. He thought he had touched her. What she wanted and who she was. Maybe something deeper had gotten scrambled in the hospital.

You might want to turn the hubs, she said, as they turned off the highway onto the Forest Service road. It looks like it's been raining.

All the modern conveniences, RL said, switching the transfer case into four high. Automatic everything.

Nice, she said.

But she didn't look nice or feel nice. She looked distracted, sick and scared. Let me help you, RL thought. Let me help you, please. They crossed a one-lane bridge across a creek and then they turned off the main gravel road onto a jeep track that branched off into the brush. Tag alder painted the sides of his truck with rainwater. They turned off twice more; and each time the road got worse, the tire tracks rutted with mud, the center grassy hump brushing against the underside of the truck. It felt unbelievable that they were not lost but Betsy clearly knew where she was going. It felt like the road was closing up behind them, like the wilderness was taking them in—a wild country that ran from here to Augusta, to Canada, north as far as north went, all dripping with rain and green.

You might want to gun it, Betsy said. This last piece is a little steep.

RL did as he was told, shoved it down into second gear and revved it up high and held on as the road twisted and bucked beneath him, a high steep washed-out gravel hillslope. He got to the top and wondered how exactly he had done so, Betsy laughing at him politely in the seat beside him.

Damn, he said, partly in having survived the ride but also in wonder at the place he found himself. It was a clearing of mud and tangled brush, nearly flat, above the forest and below the mountains. In front of him, across the wooded valley, stretched the Mission Range, jagged and white, while behind them raised the first peaks of the Swan Range and the wilderness beyond. This was not country for people, he thought. This was country for rock, snow, bears. He thought of how he had emptied out at the sight of the mountains on the drive up and now here he was in the very heart.

It started to rain again as they sat in the truck, and woodsmoke drifted across the clearing.

A garage or shed stood at the near end of the clearing, mostly finished-looking, two stories tall. A man from the Civil War stood on the second-floor porch looking down at them without expression, in a gray wool shirt-jacket and gray beard and ponytail. This was Roy. The last time RL had seen him was at their wedding, and he looked considerably different then. Across the clearing was a foundation for a house covered in several blue and gray and green plastic tarps. The plastic was dirty and leaf-stained, all but one corner, which looked to be new this year.

Out of the open doorway to the garage peered the white faces of her children.

My God, Betsy said, and started to weep, although from joy or fear or sudden sorrow RL could not tell. Her mouth was pursed into a rictus of emotion.

* * *

Across the clearing were scattered several woodpiles and several cars, among them an overgrown International Travelall and a Dodge Dart wagon with no glass in the empty sockets. Many projects had been half-started and abandoned: a log splitter, a cider press, an arbor. What was it like to be her? What was it like to call this home? Even if he had the nerve to ask, she was in no shape to answer.

Roy disappeared back into the house and then in a moment came out the ground-floor entrance and walked toward the truck. He didn't notice it was raining or at least it didn't show. He moved unhurriedly with a little hitch in his walk, some old injury.

Welcome back, he said.

Betsy stopped crying right away and tried to hide it.

He said, We missed you.

I missed you, too.

How are you?

I've been better, she said. I'm all right.

You look good, Roy said, then leaned into the open window to look at RL. Thanks for giving her the ride up, he said. I've just been kind of wrapped up here. The kids and all.

No problem, RL said.

* * *

Well, I do appreciate it, Roy said. He opened the door from the outside and held it for Betsy to get out.

She turned to RL. Aren't you going to come in? she asked. Come have a beer or a cup of coffee.

Over her shoulder RL saw the momentary flash of anger on Roy's face, no more than annoyance, really, but it sparked an answering glimmer in himself.

Sure, he said. I'll stick around. Take a little break before the drive home. Take a look around. I've never been up here before.

You're kidding.

Never.

We've been here almost twenty years, she said.

She got out of the truck and into the rain, and the children came running then and the look on her face was something RL couldn't stand to see as she hugged them close to her, standing in the pouring rain. The girl was almost as tall as her mother but long and thin, all elbows and neck, and the boy was a couple of years younger and much shorter with an unformed blank face. He looked like he was about to be born but still not ready.

This was too much to see, the look on Betsy's face and the two children wrapped around her, and RL made himself look away. Then made himself look back. She saw it, too, that moment of recognition. You do love, he thought. You do, too.

* * *

Inside was curiously dark despite big windows which let in big views of the Mission Range. It was all one long room upstairs and RL waited for his eyes to clear into the half dark. Now that they had touched her, the children would not let Betsy go. Roy stayed behind them in the barn downstairs on some errand of his own, and when RL could see the upstairs he understood why: it looked like the aftermath of a frat party in there, clothes and sweatshirts, empty bottles and dirty dishes. He sent a thought out to his daughter, then, to Layla far away, to say, *Not for you, not this, let you be spared this.* It was not just dirt and disorder that he saw here but concentrated misery, the answer to the question *What would happen if I just let go?* This, RL thought. This is what happens.

Momma's fine, Betsy whispered. Momma's going to be just fine.

The children clung to her. Betsy was in her space now, her corner of the kitchen: a soft space. Fabric all around and scraps of cotton wool, a soft light from the big window, a big worktable and a drawer full of scissors, needles, skeins of wool. Everything in reach, everything in control. The chair itself was oak with woven, Mexican-looking cushions, worn threadbare to white in places and the wood scarred and stained. Everything within reach had been worn smooth with touch, and RL wondered if that was what had happened to her son, too, that half-formed, half-finished look. . . . In the soft light from the window they all looked beautiful but unreal, like somebody's idea or a scene from a movie. Betsy was weeping but trying to stop. The girl looked angry. The boy looked like nothing at all, like water.

Betsy said, There's a beer in the refrigerator, I bet.

RL just wanted to leave. This whole business—bringing her here, this whole trip—was a mistake. Abandoned to her own life.

But somebody needed to bring her here; she couldn't drive herself.

Thanks, he said, and opened the refrigerator door: mustard, celery, some half-empty jars of jam and a half-gallon of milk that RL was certain was empty. And beer, plenty of beer, at least half of a case left in the bottom. Milwaukee's Best. RL took one anyway, opened it and took the first rank draft.

Do you want anything?

No, no, she said. I'm fine.

RL went to the window and looked out upon the sweeping vista, miles of sky and aching white peaks. This was what he meant to do, anyway, but found himself looking instead at the collection of streaks and smears on the inside of the window, remembering the essential grubbiness of kids, the mysterious ability Layla had always had to get filthy in no time at all in a clean house, doing nothing in particular. Here it would be easier. When did it change? Again he thought of his daughter, somewhere out there on the tundra, alone. . . . Now she was neat as anything, three days on the river and she still could look pretty and put together. He was lonely without her.

When he turned away from the window, Betsy had composed herself and was pushing her children at him. This is Adam, she said, and this is Ann. Say hello to Robert.

The boy mumbled a greeting but the girl spoke clearly, long-necked, her face open and curious. She was not yet a beauty but she was on the verge, still a child but not for long. She didn't know what to do with her hands. Suddenly one of them darted out, and RL took it and shook hands with her in an oddly formal businesslike way.

Thank you for taking care of my mother, she said.

Suddenly in the half-light he saw Ann and her mother's faces next to each other, and he saw the length of her and the fineness of her bones, her long soft girl's hair, and in the two of them he saw Betsy as she had been at nineteen when he had first met her, at twenty when he had slept with her: long, delicate, pretty. Looking back from Ann to her mother, he saw—an optical illusion, it felt like, some kind of trick—the girl's face and the woman's at the same time, Betsy at nineteen, the annihilating work of time, some furious sandstorm blowing through and obliterating everything in its path. The features blunted, then erased. The Sphinx. The sadness that rushed through him was not just feeling sorry for himself, for her, for all of them but a certainty that she should have been with RL all along. He would have taken better care of her, would have been a father to this lovely girl. He knew this was wrong, even as he thought it, but he felt it solidly.

Give me a hand, he said to the girl. Let's clean up a little.

You don't have to, Betsy said. Please don't.

She really didn't want him to, it embarrassed her someplace deep, and she owed him enough. For a moment he thought that he wouldn't do it but then he saw Ann's face, unreadable, gone inside, and knew that he had to. Somebody needed to take care of them.

Come on, he said to Adam. Give us a hand.

* * *

But the boy would not stir from his mother's skirts. RL gave up on him, went to the sink and began to run hot water. He had not done this in some time. He did his own dishes with a machine, but here there was no machine. Ann, mute, went around the room collecting dirties, setting them on the stained and lifting parquet counter next to the sink. Parquet was a terrible choice for a countertop. RL could have told them that much. It would never last.

Drunk, June was coming home after Red's, Charlie's, the Flame, the Turf, the I Don't Know, Luke's, the Stockman's and the Silver Dollar closed and the Oxford quit serving liquor and went over entirely to poker, brains and eggs.

Or half drunk. June thought she had drunk herself sober, which the adult version of herself does not believe is possible but the June of that night (twenty with decent fake ID) had seen with her own eyes. The dark morning was cold enough to sober her up, anyway, somewhere around zero, with a smart stinging wind coming out of the canyon, a wind that would turn half her face numb when it picked up.

That night—it could have been any Friday, still in college, drunk and pretty, looking for something but looking in the bars where there was nothing but more of the same—if it hadn't been that one night she wouldn't even remember who she was with, an array of the same faces. June ran with the clogs-and-wool-sweaters set, but on Friday night she put on her red boots, the ones with the white stars and stitching. Smart girl acting dumb, maybe. Maybe it wasn't that bad. Who was that girl?

That night she was not going home with anybody but she was walking toward the Rattlesnake with Coy, Tiffany and Blackmore, three English majors and a Nez Percé Indian (Blackmore) who she never saw again in her life. That little duplex, so clean and so alone. Picture of her family and of sunflowers by van Gogh and a teapot and a cat. It was different then, alone but all right with it. Was she?

Crossing Pattee by the post office, a Mustang comes out of nowhere fast. The four of them are halfway across the street, talking about Van Morrison, and the red car brushes by so close that it shuts them all up, scares them, maybe six inches away from Coy, who turns on his heels as the Mustang passes and raises his fist and finger and yells, *Fuck you!*

The red Mustang stops in a sideways plunge of tire squeal and tire smoke. The smell of rubber in the cold breeze. They stand there dumb as cows.

Then the Mustang does a standing-start made-for-TV 180 and then it's coming straight at them and she's up on the curb somehow and Blackmore and Tiff, but Coy is, like, *stuck* out there in the crosswalk with the Mustang coming faster than any of them can think, and then lightly he's somehow up on the hood of the thing and the motor keeps winding up, faster as it passes with Coy up on the hood shouting, *Motherfucker, motherfucker stop.*

* * *

Which he does stop cold, a hundred feet down the street, and Coy launches off the hood and onto the dirt and dirty ice of the street, rolling over and over limp. Oh God, oh God, oh God, goes Tiffany, and Blackmore starts to curse and run down the block to where the Mustang sits still. He could fire it up and run Coy over where he sits. June stands there stuck to the sidewalk, not even cold. Down the block behind her, a girl is laughing loud. From somewhere comes the sound of breaking glass.

Then the Mustang is gone and Blackmore is kneeling by Coy and she and Tiffany are suddenly there and he might be all right or not. Motherfucker, Coy says quietly, with blood coming out of his nose. Not much blood.

Keep still, Blackmore says.

Then June's up and running back toward Higgins.

Where are you going? says Blackmore.

Find a cop, she says. I'll call one if I don't see one.

Hurry, Tiff says. Hurry!

Nobody needs to tell her and there's a cop car riding up Higgins when she gets there and she puts herself square in the middle of his lane in front of him and puts her arms out wide at her sides and yells, *Stop*, and he stops. June runs to his window and there he is.

There is Taylor, the man she will marry.

* * *

This is his face at twenty-seven: round, a little soft, with a crawling caterpillar of a mustache across his upper lip, traces of baby fat that she finds endearing at first but later she will nag him, drag him to the gym, cook him skimpy meals and flatter him until he becomes most of the chiseled cowboy she wants him to be. This is him. June knows it in a second, in a tenth of a second, in the time it takes to see a face. This is it. He doesn't even like her at first, drunk college chick, and then when he understands that this is *serious*, he's all business and quick about it. Fuck you, let's go. She points and he doesn't wait for her, sprints off down Broadway with his lights on and his siren going for all of a block and a half. Two minutes later it looks like a cop convention, their faces bathed in twirling lights and Coy still out on the pavement but he's OK—he's moving and talking. Six, eight, ten police cars all around with their lights going and their radios barking. June tells her story to a uniformed cop and then ten minutes later to a cop in a suit, and all the while she's looking for him but he's always tied up talking to somebody or on the radio and then one minute she looks around and he's just gone. . . .

All this in a moment, while she's lying next to Howard—he's sleeping, snoring sometimes. It's November. It snowed hard last night and all through the day, and now her bedroom is full of snowy light, moonlight reflected off the low-hanging clouds and the white snow, it glows through the windows. She has to be at work in five hours, she ought to be asleep, she was sleeping a minute ago but then woke up with just the two words *flashing lights* in her brain and the whole thing in an instant. It's not the whole memory, it's just a point of memory, but then the whole thing unfolds in her mind to where she can taste the night air, the exhaust from all the cop cars. Things end and never end. Somewhere in her mind it's still whole, the twenty-year-old never gone but still living, the same year over and over. . . . Who is she? All these selves, this patchwork of scar tissue and bright moments, sex and sleeping and that one dinner they had at that restaurant by the ocean in California, the fresh peas picked from the garden, steamed for a minute and then served with butter and salt, nothing else.

How did it come to this?

Outside the window, out in the soft light of the snow and dampened moonlight, the deer move down to the river to drink, breaking through the crust of snow to graze on last year's grass, stick-thin, slow-moving, deathly. What was it like? to live in the present, always, or in the never? . . . Dogs remembered, she was almost sure of it. Dogs dreamed, she knew it. But it wasn't this kind of half here, half anywhere that she was, part memory and part desire and never exactly *here* except when she was asleep—and even then, the dreaming . . .

Snow on the ground, and more on the way. A stranger sleeping beside her. She could feel it coming.

To be whole, to be present, to be on horseback over the white fields and deadfall limbs at full gallop, fast, no time but the now, just the gesture, the line between horse and rider and running all blurry and nothing outside the moment, no dreams no memories no desire just the speed itself and the woman disappearing into the speed. To be the horse itself. To be nothing. To be the moment, the running itself and nothing more, not even a trace, like the breath on a mirror . . .

*

Forty-one degrees and the wind howling out of
Wolf Creek, blowing shifting corduroy lines across the gray water,
water reflecting gray skies and hills, the occasional solitary ponderosa pine or juniper, a patch of blue sky sledding across the far
edge of the sky, the morning lowering toward afternoon, the ten-
minute project to get a cigar lit. This was fun.

This was something. Maybe just trying to prove something to
somebody, maybe to himself. The cast was off now and this was
what Edgar had always loved, alone and the river, trying to out-
smart an animal whose brain was just a wide spot in its spinal column. Treachery and stealth and cunning, though, that all made it
sound worse than it was. Mostly he threw them back. Today he had
promised to bring one back for Amy. That was something, too, he
thought, looking at the run edge of his cigar where the wind had

blown the ash uneven: the bloodlust of women, the way they wanted meat for themselves and their children. Layla was the only girl he knew who understood catch-and-release, and even then she seemed reluctant. All the little girls with blood on their lips and fingers, it gave him an idea for a drawing. Maybe a painting. Maybe a nice big painting that nobody would like and nobody would buy, the same as ever.

Nicotine and cynical, like a horse and carriage . . . He drew on the cigar again, but it burned hot and raw with the run down its side. Doused it in the water for a long half minute and then threw it up on the bank, as far as he could. It was only leaf, only poison. It would decompose.

Edgar turned his attention to the water again. Under the wind-ripple he could sense a seam, a place where water came together with slower water, where a big fish could fin easy in the current. He would be a foot or eighteen inches deep or maybe deeper or maybe anywhere or completely imaginary. His mind felt like a typewriter turning over the possibilities, something automatic. This was what he loved. He had to remind himself.

This hypothetical big fish would be feeding on what? On anything—it was impossible to say. A mayfly nymph in late autumn. A take-out cheeseburger. Edgar found it hard to concentrate.

Marriage was the thing he would not think about.

A bead-head lightning bug on the point and a pink scud on the dropper. The wind tried to blow his hat off. It wasn't just chilly but cold, the coming winter, or maybe the winter just arriving. The long grass whipping in the breeze. He tied a yarn strike indicator, pink and orange like a clown wig, and tried a cast with the wind at his back. He could feel his back cast sucking as it hit the air and then his forward cast came whizzing by his ear completely out of control and landed the whole apparatus in the water, line, flies and bozo wig, with the grace of a full set of plumber's tools. The hypothetical fish took off for New Orleans.

Edgar considered the possibility that his life was not tragic but instead comic, that he was just another joker making a mess of things, an example for others. In his clown suit, his waders and boots, his many-pocketed vest with the many objects dangling and his humorous fingerless gloves . . .

The lines of her face. The line of her jaw. He remembered tracing it in the soft light of the shop. Now he couldn't seem to stop himself; by now he had made two dozen small drawings of her face, and a few paintings as well. Mostly they looked like her, though a few devolved into geometry, color fields. But mainly just her face when she told him about Russia, about the siege, about the cannibal markets and sawdust bread and the corpses left to freeze in the streets from October right up into May. Also her face in repose and even in happiness and mockery when a man from New Jersey came into the rainy shop and wanted to know where the fishin' was hot. Her happiness in quiet: a cup of tea, rain on the window glass, the swish of passing traffic, Edgar's company. She could make him happy. Edgar knew it, hip-deep in the Missouri. He could make Layla happy as well.

This is what is meant to be a man, he thought: to suffer, to be steadfast, to be stoic in the face of happiness. Not happiness, just possibility. Baby girl, little Olive, another baby on the way, that was the real joy—and it was, he wasn't talking himself into anything.

And if things had been a little slow, a little sad with Amy, that was just the way things were. *Postpartum*, there was even a name for it. He wasn't talking himself into anything. Olive, her little face shining up at him. Nothing artificial about that, nothing sentimental, a good solid ax-handle feeling, well-worn and well used. And if he didn't exactly know where things were with Amy, that wasn't the end of the world. They had time to work things out. They would have this next baby and then, when things settled out a little, maybe they would go on a nice trip. Amy's mother could watch the babies—she'd offered a dozen times.

He looked at the water, flat and gray in the gray light. Winter was here, not hard winter yet but still the flat light and cold wind. They could go to Mexico, to somewhere on the ocean, drink beer and get a sunburn. They could be together and be happy. Him and Amy, is what he meant to say. Edgar and his wife.

*

Dorris MacKintyre raised sheep up by Ovando for fifty years. He bought a cabin and seventy-five hundred acres for a dollar an acre when he inherited money from his father in the 1930s, mountain land and high sage flats, not good for much. Later the federals came and bought the mountain half of it back from him and that was now part of the Bob Marshall Wilderness. Any time you drove over to Great Falls and you looked up at the mountains, that was his land. Used to be his.

Got married to a gal he met at a nightclub in Black Eagle at the 3 D Ballroom where they used to have Negro bands. Good girl. She was just out with her friends for a good time.

Had four kids, all girls. Every time he had another girl, he added another room onto the cabin, one for the marriage and one each for the girls, so now that little cabin was halfway to a hillbilly mansion. Never had any money. Land-rich and cash-poor. Not that the land was ever worth that much, up at forty-five hundred feet and no moisture to speak of. Frozen up half the time. Just getting the girls off to school was an adventure. Getting them and Trudy to church. They had a service in Ovando, but they had it at the bar and Trudy couldn't go along with that, so they drove to Lincoln every Sunday.

One of the girls, Joy, it turned out she had a congenital heart defect. There was no way anybody could have known, it was just, one day on the playground at school, that was that. Trudy never really got over it. Not all the way. How would you?

Now Dorris lies in a bed by the window in his daughter's house in Missoula, a metal invalid bed with a back that inclines and reclines electrically. His hands lie on the white bedspread like stumps of wood, brown and weathered, liver spotted and lumpy. Since the stroke they do not work as well. There's a TV at the foot of the bed, but it's not usually on. Dorris was never around them enough to get used to the racket. He would watch a little baseball once in a while but now the Series is over and if there's one thing he can't stand it's football. His granddaughter is in and out after middle school, and she's the thing that's keeping him alive still. Dorris can't believe that she and he are flesh and blood, little Greta, a quarter Blackfoot Indian. She pleases him no end. He just can't get over her, with her black hair and her red lips and her twenty earrings. The things her mother lets her get away with. The clothes! Sometimes Dorris has to look away, just to keep from seeing his granddaughter's little tits.

* * *

Most days it's pretty quiet in the back room. Lisa, his daughter, is away at the title company where she works. Greta's in school. Greta's dad is pushing up sand in Saudi Arabia. The great wide world is bustling by outside. Lisa thinks he ought to have somebody home with him all the time, but Dorris doesn't want this. He likes these hours alone, him and the squirrels. He watches them against the gray sky, walking on the telephone lines, chasing each other up and down the big maple tree out back. The time to just sit and watch squirrels. Dorris won't last the winter.

He's all right with that.

One of these good old days, when everybody's at work or at school or otherwise hurrying through their day, when the fire trucks are rushing off to save somebody and the grocery drivers are backing their semis up to the loading dock of the Food Farm a block away, one of these days when Greta's sitting in social studies and the kids from the U are talking about whatever the hell they talk about over cups of coffee in Bernice's—whatever it is, it means a lot to them—and the carpenters are pounding nails on a roof in the half-assed snow, when the new loaves of bread are coming out of the oven and bankers are stealing and the people on the city council are out taking bribes, sometimes he thinks it might be in the afternoon but he's pretty sure it'll be in the morning, right when everybody's getting a good push on the day, hitching up their britches and getting to work, Dorris is just going to lie on back in the bed and that will be that.

He can already feel it, like something he's done a thousand times before. Pound a nail or tie a trucker's hitch.

* * *

June, the gal from the hospice, brought him a tape of the angel music and she says it'll make things easier, but Dorris doubts it. It would just be contrary to his luck. He would put the tape on, he could just see it, and lie on back in the bed. And then forty-five minutes later the tape would be over and he would just be lying there with his thumb up his ass.

No thanks. He'll take his chances.

The thing Dorris likes these days are the squirrels. The bed is set up in the back room on the alleyway, and it's quiet back here. He's got names for them and all, nothing too original. The one with the black markings around his nose, for instance, Dorris calls him Blackie. But you just look at them, you quit taking them for granted for a change, and these squirrels are pretty amazing. The death-defying way they walk across a telephone line. The high-speed fights across the fence tops and off into the trees! Dorris can't tell if they're fighting for real or just playing. Blackie and Karen, Spot and Leroy and Ferdinand—Dorris calls him Ferdinand because he's the bull squirrel, the one that's always chasing after the others. Tough life, Dorris thinks, being the badass squirrel. Bigger balls and more nuts than any of the other squirrels. Dorris has known a few people like that.

He gets restless sometimes, and when he does, he cleans his guns. He laughs at himself sometimes to think of it. Cleanest guns in western Montana. And what the hell is he going to do with them? The only thing he could shoot from here was the squirrels and Dorris isn't about to start hunting squirrels. Still, he gets the brushes out and the gun oil and he disassembles them slowly with shaking hands: his service revolver, the 30.06 with the good scope, the 45–70 buffalo gun that he got from his father. It would about knock him down to fire the thing even when he was good to go. A beast of a gun. Who would ever use it again? The girls were scattered from here to San Diego, and the two boys among the grandkids were soft little suburban kids. Dorris loved them as much as any of the rest, but he couldn't help wishing they were different, wishing they were *interested*. He took them out killing gophers a few years back, when they were nine and ten, took them to a hayfield on the old Lindbergh place that was nothing but gopher holes from one end to the other and gave them each a .22 rifle and a box of shells and both of them quit before that first box ran out. A kid who didn't like killing gophers. Dorris didn't even want to understand.

*

A patch of quick sunlight raced across the brown grass, a sudden outburst, bright and blinding, and with it an upwelling of spring. He knew in his dark place that she would live to see the green grass and feel the sunlight, a little secret of hope in the dark of December. It was just a small chance, but a small chance was all she needed if it worked. And if she was right—and RL thought she was crazy but that didn't mean he couldn't go along with her—if she was right and it was all about the positive mental energy, then maybe his small little glimmer of positive energy would be enough to put the whole business over the top. He wanted her to live. He was surprised how much.

There was one place where the grass was still green for some reason and when the sunlight hit that, it just exploded into green light.

* * *

He was smoking a little Swiss cigar and waiting for her to come out of the oncologist's, leaning up against a bench, watching a frozen waterfall, under a big No Smoking Within 50 Feet of Building sign. Invisible speakers were piping the local country station into the courtyard. In principle RL was in favor of country music, but in practice it all sounded the same. Much of his life seemed to be like this: a thing he ought to want but really didn't.

He was thinking about mayflies, the way some of them are born without even mouths. They live their day in the sun and they breed and they fall back as spinners to the water. Nothing sad about it.

*

Layla wakes up bolt upright at three in the morning, covered in dreams. This time it's June's wedding, spring sunshine and white roses, an afternoon on the green, green grass. Who
is this groom? Layla never quite sees his face, always turned away at
the last moment, always with his back to her, though she's curious
enough. She sees his back in tuxedo black, leaning into a circle of
men all in black like crows, and laughter and smoke coming out of
the circle.

June is dressed like June exactly, a wedding dress in white and
lace yet somehow still businesslike, her practical short hair and a
cocktail-length skirt, if Layla has that right, which she imagines she
doesn't. June is running June's wedding, fussing around, arranging,
ordering her friends around just like herself. Her eyes keep scan-
ning right by where Layla's standing but she never seems to see her,

which makes Layla feel ghostly, invisible, creepy. When she was little, Layla used to imagine what it was like to be the ghost at your own funeral, watching all the people you knew and all the people you loved in their black clothes and tears, missing you gone and you right there but just unable to let them know, that invisible screen between one world and the next . . . but this was a happy time, or supposed to be. The thing that's weird about the wedding is that Layla doesn't seem to know anybody. They all look familiar enough, a little underdressed, a little sunburned, radiating good health and outdoor pursuits and stories of big fish and backcountry powder caches—these are the people Layla knows, their ways and morals, their habits and importancies, but while she knows these people well in general she doesn't know any of these people in particular. June is getting married among strangers.

And Layla can't find a way through to her. June's eyes keep passing by her without recognition. Layla is a stranger here, and June is getting married among strangers, people who don't know her and won't take care of her as they ought to. Even now, even awake, Layla feels the sadness of it: the temporary home disbanded, scattered to the winds, and now this friendless place. The guests all *seem* like June's friends, but they are not June's friends, just people who look like them. People who look like me, Layla thinks. Where is my mother? I need my mother.

In her usual little bed, the rain dripping through the trees outside. No wonder she's depressed! Also, she's almost sure she's pregnant. Her period—regular as Old Faithful in normal times—is three and a half weeks late, and she wants chocolate all the time. She wants to go back to sleep, back to that wedding if she can. Because strange as it is, foreign, she can still remember the sunlight on her skin, the look of soft grass and green leaves and little white clouds scuffing along in the blue sky, a place of pleasure and warmth, the tables laden with good food and cold white wine, the laughter and murmur of friendly conversation. Only later, when she is half asleep again, does she remember the brown around the stems of the grapes, the petals already turning, the flies—one by one—in love with all that sugar, and all the spilled wine. They couldn't stay away.

*

What they didn't talk about was everything, children, Roy, dirty dishes and the eve of chemotherapy. There was, at this point, no point. Her little unhappy face in the candlelight. Halfway through dinner he was ready for all this to stop, he'd had enough, too much: for all her trying, she could not conceal her entire lack of possibility. No straws to clutch at, no parachute on the burning airplane. The pope, a hippie, and Henry Kissinger . . .

What?

Nothing, RL said. He didn't realize that he had said anything out loud. Maybe he hadn't. Betsy was spooky that way.

I want to go to Hawaii, she said. Thailand, anyplace warm.

* * *

Orlando, RL said.

I'd settle for Orlando, she said. I don't even know where this comes from. It's like the way you suddenly want chocolate or something.

Or whiskey.

I'd settle for whiskey.

You might have to tonight, RL said. Supposed to snow all night. That airport is *closed*.

I don't have any money anyway.

The waiter came and took their plates away, RL's polished and empty—a rack of lamb which had been all tasty morsels and no real meat—and Betsy's plate on which the food had been pushed around but only halfheartedly eaten. She wasn't crazy about it. Or maybe she just didn't like the idea of food. Maybe she was alive on some other kind of nutriment, the song of unseen angels or the mysterious radiation of the sun. Ashes, RL thought. Ashes and diamonds, diamonds and rust.

My boy Edgar is taking a group down to Bimini after the first of the year, he said. It's almost enough to piss a guy off.

Why him and not you?

Oh, RL said. He was the one who hustled up the customers. I don't even think he'll end up getting paid for it. It's just a free trip to Bimini.

* * *

Betsy looked up. It had been partly about her, why he hadn't gone, and she knew it just by looking at him.

Plus, you know, he said. First of the year. Taxes and all.

I bet, she said.

OK, so she didn't believe him. A little gleam of mischief. Still capable of laughter.

What? he said.

You are semitransparent, she said. You should come milk goats with me sometimes. You'd like the goats, I think. They're a little unpredictable, always surprising, like cats and deer and daughters. I wasn't ever meant for this.

She sweeps her arm around the restaurant, its small lights and murmured conversations. A table of drunk New West business types—sunglasses on little strings around their necks—goes off in laughter at somebody's punch line.

You're going to think this is crazy, Betsy said.

What?

Something, she said, a dog or maybe a coyote or even a wolf—Roy thought it might have been a wolf—anyway, something got into the goats one night while we were asleep. We keep them penned up, you know. It's just to keep them together—there's a little shed but it's just a wire fence, nothing that would keep anything out. We just woke up and there was this screaming—it sounded just like a baby screaming. You remember that sound?

Worst thing in the world.

Worst thing ever, she said. It goes right through you. . . . Whatever it was, was gone by the time Roy got his gun and made it out there, but Buck Henry was dead on the ground and two of the does were just standing there with their throats ripped out. I saw it. I came right behind him.

That sounds bad enough, RL said. Lucky it wasn't a bear.

That's what Roy said.

She picked up her glass of red wine and sipped at it and then drank from it more purposefully, a long draft.

This isn't the time or place for a story like this, she said. I thought it was something else when I started.

What happened?

He shot them, Robert. Right while I was standing there watching. He says he had to, I don't know. Maybe he's right. I didn't even have the chance to say good-bye, I just had to run back into the house and keep the kids from seeing that.

She was crying, tears standing in her eyes.

You see? It's stupid, stupid. They were just goats, just animals. You buy them out of the paper for thirty dollars.

* * *

You loved them.

Yes, I did.

There's nothing stupid about that.

Maybe not, she said. But then I ended up in therapy, I just couldn't shake it. Couldn't stop thinking about it, you know? A year and a half at seventy-five dollars an hour and we didn't even have insurance. It turns out I'm a complicated person.

I could have told you that for free.

That's what everybody says.

She reassembled herself out of bits of tissue paper and solemn expression, wiping the sorrow from her face.

Don't get me started, she said.

He could save her from this, he thought. He could save both of them. The great escape, out of the disaster of her life, the endless sameness of his own. They would not have forever, he knew that. They might not have long. But they would not need forever, just a moment. He could touch her. She could make him happy. It seemed so simple, just for a moment. No more dead goats and ex-wives. He felt a part of something holy. Something larger than himself. He felt quite suddenly light, rising out of his body. He was smiling at her, at the sheer pleasure of her presence, which was not right.

* * *

What is it? Betsy asked.

But for the moment he was too wrought up to answer, too tangled and pure. A happiness not his own and not hers but arising out of the air between them. The idea of her. The possibility of escape.

Escape: he didn't know he needed to, not until that moment. Didn't know he wanted it. Then suddenly the getaway was everything to him, every waking thought and fancy. They could not exist here, in the daylight world. They could not be together. But somewhere under palm trees, or in the Spanish sun—he always connected happiness and daylight, someplace warm and bright and not here. Food and wine, laughter. Winter was coming. But maybe not for them.

An act of violence. Cut the knot. He had it in him. Did she?

He dreamed that she did. Dreamed it before this moment, but it was just now coming true, a thing that had been growing in him, there in the dark, ready to burst out. He knew her. He knew what was next.

Midnight, whiskey. They were side by side on the sofa, neither one of them talking. RL was thinking about last times, and about airports.

The way you never knew it was the last time until it had already happened, and then it was too late.

The way the air itself in airports must wear out from all the coming and going, all the love and loss and parting and greeting, embracing, tearful kisses.

He misses his daughter, yes, he does. Some fearful premonition. Or maybe just death herself sitting on the couch next to him, sipping her Bushmills and thinking about whatever she was thinking about. Her hands were thin and rough, skeletal where they wrapped around the icy glass. It happened to everybody, worse when you worked as much as she did. His own hands—RL looked at them in the air in front of him—were honorably messed up, he felt. Work, adventure, injury. He knuckles were scarred as a boxer's.

It was those fucking trailers is what it was. Every time he got within ten feet of a trailer hitch.

Something about the public place, the expected thing. Everyone was coming and going, saying hello and saying good-bye to the people they loved. The rough edges of the individual person got sanded away and all that was left was the smooth impersonal outline of a feeling. All these emotions and we're all having them. Like you knew what you were supposed to do. RL wanted that, wanted to be emptied out, wanted to watch television and listen to soothing music from high, invisible speakers. He just didn't know what he was supposed to do here. Give me a script, he thought, a line to walk. Don't make me improvise.

She said, When did everything get so grim?

Like what?

I don't know, she said, and sipped her whiskey—Bushmills neat, a glass of water by her side. Between the whiskey and the wine, she had already had more than she should have. The next morning would start at five thirty.

Good-bye, good-bye.

* * *

She said, I feel like I went up on my mountaintop and everything was OK, you know? Not OK—things were bad, but people were out there trying. I just feel like people aren't trying anymore, they won't look for anything different. It's just like, take your place in line, you know? Get a job, watch TV.

RL was thinking about that half-finished basement, the faces of the children peering out from the unlit garage into the rain.

OK, she said, reading his mind. Nobody's life is perfect.

This seemed like an understatement. He kept his trap shut.

Don't, she said.

What?

Don't judge me.

I'm not trying to.

No, I know, she said. I'm doing the same, you know? or at least I'm trying. That's what I do, you know. Judge, judge, judge. That's what I'm good at.

It was strange to hear her be so completely right about herself. He was used to hearing her wrong, telling him all about how she was completely some way, when really she wasn't at all.

I haven't said a word about your pickup truck.

* * *

It's true.

Despite the fact that it gets like, what? twelve miles to the gallon. You use it to drive yourself around. One person.

You're falling off the wagon here a little.

Indulge me, she said. Maybe I feel like it. Maybe it all just looks a little stupid to me. It feels good once in a while, you know, just to sit back and rant.

My house.

It's awfully big for just one person. What does it cost you to heat?

There are two of us here, he said.

Now.

Now is all I'm talking about.

What?

By way of answer, he reached across the kitchen table and drew her to him and she came, surprised at first, a moment's reluctance but then willingly, sat across his lap and let herself be kissed on the mouth. Did not let herself. Gave herself. Kissed him then and held him and RL felt the kitchen loosen and drift, a small boat on big water.

* * *

This is not a good idea, she whispered into his neck.

I know.

I have children.

I know, I know, I know, he said.

*

June was awake for some reason but she didn't know why. Quarter to one in the morning by the bedside clock. Something.

She had lived alone for many years and was not afraid of the small noises of a house at night, an old house like this one that creaked and grumbled in the wind and the cold and the summer heat. This was something else. What? Howard was in Portland, drinking. June was alone in her house and the world was far away and shrinking.

There it went again. A sound out of the kitchen maybe.

Rosco puking blood on the kitchen floor.

* * *

She was out the door with the dog in her arms in one continuous movement, clothes to car keys to glasses to blanket, a good wool blanket that would be spoiled now with blood and dog shit. Blind with pain, Rosco tried to bite her hand. She settled him into the backseat and tucked the blanket around his thin legs.

Do not die, she said to him.

He looked at her with big sorrowful eyes. He would live if she made him. He didn't necessarily want it for himself. A dog's life.

Don't, she said.

What she meant was don't stop, don't stop, don't stop breathing, but he was just a dog, he wouldn't understand, and so she pushed her old Subaru up to seventy on the curves by the cemetery and prayed there was no ice on the road. Found herself *praying*. All her life, she had preached calm to the dying, she'd tried to bring them to peace, and now when it was her turn—not even a father or a sister but a *dog*—she found that calm had deserted her and a clockwork panic going off in her chest, hurry! Down the icy deserted Walmart parking lot, the rendering plant, the police station and the plumbing supply, all the filth and ugliness, the secondhand cars parked in crusts of black snow. I flunk, she thought. I suck. Wondered for a moment if she was dreaming this.

Rosco bit her again as she gathered him in his blanket from the backseat of the car, drew blood this time so his blood and hers stained the blanket together. Stood ringing the emergency bell of the vet hospital, willing them to hurry. A sleep-stained tech let her in and took the dog from her, blanket and all, into the mystery rooms at the back. June was left alone and bleeding on the linoleum of the waiting room floor.

A pot of coffee sat among magazines at one end of the waiting room. She tried a cup, but the coffee had been sitting on the warmer all day and night and it was bitter, black and concentrated. She spat her sip back into the paper cup and then threw the cup away.

Golf Digest. Cat Fancy. BusinessWeek.

She took her cell phone from her coat pocket and looked at it and wondered why there was nobody to call. Nobody who knew the dog enough to care. She thought of Layla, out in Seattle. Howard in his motel room, if he was even back to his motel by this time of night. Once every month or two he would drive or fly to Portland, where he once lived, and he would get drunk there, and stay drunk for the weekend. He didn't touch a drop otherwise, and he didn't drive while he was there. This all seemed reasonable in a way that creeped June out, but she kept her mouth shut about it. Really, it wasn't any of her business.

I was not meant for this life, she thought. She could do it, she could make it through alone, take the little hand grenades life threw at her. She was a strong person. But it was not the life she was meant for.

She dialed RL's number and listened to it ring unanswered in the empty room. The loneliest sound she knew.

*

RL stood in the guest room doorway and watched the slow rise and slow fall of her sleeping back in the tiny light of the moon. Slim, white, pretty shoulders, the curve down to her hip, it could have been a girl's body. The rot and death inside.

Heard his telephone ringing in the kitchen.

It was strange how much of her was still good, how much remained of the girl. She went from waking to sleep instantly, without worry or sweat, the way Layla would run till she dropped on a summer night. . . . Her breath was sweet and slow, and she moved, gentle underwater movements. RL felt something big and cumbersome moving around inside him. She was not going to make it, were the odds. She was not going to live. And all this unlived life, all the years stuck in Purgatory with her knitting needles and her garden, the faces of the children in the rain . . . This longing to undo, untangle, revisit, reset. This *futility*.

He closed the door again as silently as he could and went back to his chair in the living room, his little glass of Johnnie Walker on the rocks, his empty nest. He missed his daughter, yes, he did.

The little pagan children spent eternity in Purgatory because they were without sin but they had not been baptized. This seemed like an argument against God. When he was a boy, he had cried for these children. When he was a boy, he had never cried at all. How long had it been? Motherless, abandoned. Who was that on the telephone? 2:13.

He would save her. Out of the alcohol, stupor and half sleep came certainty. Not save her from the big thing but from the futility. He felt himself dive down into the blackness, under the surface, down where Betsy was. He would bring her back up into the light, if only for a moment. Down in the foul black brown sticky place where she was. Down and back up again. He would do it. He would. Alive and in the sunshine, somewhere warm, somewhere pleasure, somewhere drinks and ease and water to swim in. Things were hard for her and RL himself was a hard man and life felt hard all the time and just a minute of soft, just a minute. A little breather. He finished his drink and went off to bed, a man with a mission.

*

The ferry pulled away from Anacortes, slowly at first, with a big diesel groan and much white water laced and boiled against the steel barriers of the dock. It was raining, three thirty, fading toward nightfall. Green shaggy forest islands slipped past them, slowly at first, in and out of the mist and cloud. Every lit building looked like home, warm and yellow.

Homeless, Layla thought. She turned to Edgar.

What am I supposed to be? she asked.

A friend, I guess, he said. A model. A supermodel.

They know you, though, right? The people who run the gallery?

* * *

A friend of my parents, Edgar said. He gave me my first show.

I shouldn't be here, she said. I really shouldn't.

They watched the water for a moment without talking, watching the town ease away, the lonely departure. The lights of town were bright already in the fading afternoon and it was just the two of them out on the deck, a cold damp wind that only got colder as the boat picked up speed and left the land behind. Going, going, gone, she thought.

I wanted to see you, Edgar said.

I'm cold, she said. Let's go inside.

The passenger deck was warmer than the outside and neon-lit with island hippies and business types and wives in Polarfleece and Gore-Tex, everybody with money, nobody sick or poor. Even the tattoos on the punk girls look expensive, sharp and fresh. As opposed to Montana barfly tattoos, the blue smear that once said Charlene . . . It smelled like rainwater on linoleum, cafeteria grease, elementary school in the rain. Some hot chocolate, maybe, a doughnut might be good. The stuffy heat in here and the cold wind outside. Salmon swimming somewhere deep under the ferry, she could feel them. The child swimming inside her. She had not told Edgar yet. She wasn't sure she was going to.

Do you want something to drink? he asked. They have beer, I think.

No, she thought, but she said yes. Took a seat in a booth by the window and looked out at the darkening water, looking for seal heads and seeing only gulls and distant tankers. A white sail in the gray afternoon, far off. It was the time of day when she could see the water outside and the reflection of the lit-up passenger deck behind her at the same time in the glass and it was hard to say which one was real. Confession, she thought, penance. Her mother, in one of her occasional bursts of motherhood, had stopped drinking and stopped taking drugs except for smoking pot and started going to different churches. She even had a job for a while. Layla would have been eight or nine. She spent some weekends and then even week-nights with Dawn in her little house by the railroad tracks. An improvised quality to their lives, a sense that neither one of them knew where they were going, what they were doing—it made life exciting. Layla missed it sometimes, the feeling when she woke up that she never knew where the day would take her. One day she was dancing with the Sufis, the next day she was praying the rosary. But it was 6 a.m. Mass that Layla remembered, the women in damp wool, the lingering incense in the shadows, midwinter dark that was still not quite daylight when the Mass let out . . . and the smell of wet on linoleum, melted snow.

A nice strong ale for a rainy day, said Edgar, setting down a pair of brimming cups. This will put hair on your chest.

But I don't want hair on my chest.

Then it won't, he said.

Loud, false. He was not himself. Not the considerate, gentle man who had slept in her tiny bed the night before, cupped together against the cold and damp. Now her roommates knew, which was all right, Layla guessed. She was done with Daniel any-way, or he was done with her. But where was gentle Edgar?

* * *

The one she loved.

She didn't see a problem with the word, though she had never said it to him, never said it like that. I loved that movie. I'd love some more wine. But never I love you. Never to a lover, to Daniel, to anyone.

I can't believe I live here, she said. Look at that! It's not even four in the afternoon.

Now she was false, too. False and false. The happy pretend couple. They stared out at the water and saw only their faces reflected back at them in the glass, blue in the neon. He looked sorrowful and confused and then she remembered that she was the reason for his sorrow and confusion and she hardened against him again. Leave me alone, then.

I lived in Olympia once, he said. Went to get my shoes off the closet floor one morning and there was green mold all over them. That was pretty much that.

We talk and we talk and we talk and we never say what we mean.

Edgar looked like he had been slapped—stunned, then angry. There was a little satisfaction in that, at least.

What do you want to know? he said. Just ask me. Anything.

OK: what am I doing here?

* * *

Maybe I'm not the person to ask, he said. I wanted you to come to my opening with me. I asked if you would. Look, I want what I want, you know? If you think I shouldn't ask, then I won't next time.

That's not what I mean.

Well, what do you mean, then?

I don't know, she said. I really don't. I just feel like we got into this mess because it made us happy and now we're both unhappy all the time. All the time! I mean, I think of you and it makes me happy but everything around it.

I know.

And you have all the power, she said. You make all the decisions. I'm just along for the ride.

That's not fair.

Well, you tell me, then. Tell me how it is.

Edgar didn't say anything, just held onto his beer glass with his cold, thin hand and looked out the window at the passing ships, the cabins and little clusters of town lights. And all she had to do was reach across the table and take his hand and things would be all right again, she knew it. He wore an old gray sweater that she knew had a hole in the armpit, scuffed boots and jeans to his own opening. She loved that sweater. Still she could not bring herself. They traveled across the dark water as strangers.

*

A punch line, except that it was no joke: thirty-nine years old, slim and strong. Taylor had been out in the mountains on his bicycle, a nice old Ritchey that was still hanging in the rafters of the garage, waiting for him to come back. Felt the first pangs or pains a few miles up the Rattlesnake, turned around and rode it out, made it into the trailhead where somebody had a cell phone and called 911 on himself.

June was at work that day on the OB ward five stories above the emergency room, but she didn't find out for an hour and by then Taylor was dead. It wouldn't have mattered. They told her he crashed in the ambulance on the way back and never really came around after that, though he was still alive by a thread when they got him in and that still bothers her. Even if he didn't know, maybe he would have known just the touch of her hand. It's one of those thoughts she knows she should leave alone but she can't seem to; five in the morning, just light out, and June lying in her bed alone and thinking about a thing that happened in another life . . . What if she could have that moment back?

It didn't really matter. A minute more or less. Some people never in their lives knew love. They had years. But what if she had known?

Around and around and around.

Her life is going backward now. From the present moment, which seems so insubstantial that it might not even exist, back into the days when she was nothing but a thought, a feeling, a suffering, the year after the funeral in which she lay on the carpet of the living room with Rosco just to feel the warmth of another living body beside hers and Rosco—a young dog then, lean and handsome— consented to lie with her, without end, did not move until she let him know that it was all right to. She's just a script now, a set of intentions and directions. Back then, she was an accident, all chance. But before that, she was real, she had a body and a husband and together they had ventured up the Bitterroot to look at a litter of Golden pups and found him in a trailer that smelled of Clorox. The women who bred and raised him were each recently divorced and one of them had cancer and a solitary horrible parrot sat in the corner. It was like the world was in three dimensions then and now it was flattened out, a drawing. There had been two parrots that the breeder was watching for a girl in a wheelchair, and one of the par- rots had died and she was going to replace it—the girl was nearly blind, she'd never know—but then it seemed like the girl was likely to die herself and so there was no point in buying another. Besides, the breeder said, the parrots were horrible to the girl. All they did was peck at her and make her bleed.

The breeder was so big and unhealthy that she wheezed trying to get from one side of the room to the other and bending down to pick a pup was almost beyond her, but the dogs themselves were glowing and lively and pretty. She gave one pup to Taylor and one to June and that one was Rosco. June knew it the moment she touched him. Them there eyes.

They both felt death hovering above that trailer, waiting to strike. They both felt anxious, waiting for the day when they could come pick him up; and then, when the day came, they felt that they had rescued him from that death.

Taylor had been driving through L.A. once a few years before this—still in college, maybe, she thought—and had gotten himself pulled over, mistaken for somebody else, and these asshole L.A. cops had him spread-eagled on the hood of his car with a nightstick up between his legs and they were yelling at him, Motherfucker, motherfucker where's the rosco? Taylor didn't even know what they meant by it, but they didn't stop till they'd searched his whole car, half an hour in the sun with his cheek on the hood of his car.

So they named the dog Rosco.

Taylor had been in L.A. trying to break into the jazz scene. Trombone was his first love, his only love. Everybody else was listening to the Blues Magoos and Jimi Hendrix, and he was up in his second-floor bedroom in Hamilton, Montana, listening to "Chasing the Trane" and "Ornithology." He was smart in his body, not so much in his mind. Never saw him with a book in his hand. RL was a little like that, too. Taylor, as soon as she was ready to settle down with a novel and a glass of wine—God, she drank some awful cheap wine back then—he'd be off to the garage with a wrench in his hand, ready to fix something or break something. He had a room in the basement, too, which he had lined with old mattresses and rugs with a record player in it and he would go down there with his trombone and practice and June would have to pretend she didn't hear it. Really, he was a good player but just a solo trombone with none of the other parts got old. It wasn't so bad in summer but in December when she was stuck inside.

Taylor wanted to name him Bird so he could have a dog named Bird, but June thought you didn't want to confuse a dog anymore than you had to. So Rosco. Rosco because it was a little bit danger-ous just from the L.A. business and they had beaten danger to get him home with them.

Then he got sick. The third day they had him home, he started puking blood in the morning, and had bloody diarrhea.

Taylor said it, but June knew instantly in her heart what he meant when he said they had called this on themselves. Some creepy magic, as if they had named him Bird and he had flown away. Sitting in the linoleum room waiting to hear. They brought the puppy tiny and barely alive in a blanket and Taylor held him to his chest and Rosco couldn't hold himself, a stream of brown liquid shit and red blood down the front of Taylor's shirt. It was parvo, the vet said, we'll give him an IV and keep him quiet and hope for the best. The two of them in the bar that night praying to whatever they could find to pray to, knowing they had called this on themselves, the little helpless pup paying for their failings. It wasn't fair. He hadn't done anybody wrong. He was just a little fellow who meant nobody harm. He was a good dog.

If he made it through that first night.

That's what the vet said.

Which he did. All this long life, all these days and deer chasing and morning sunlight on the kitchen floor and it hung by a thread that first night, but hang it did. The thread held. The dog lived, thirteen years until tomorrow. We dodged a bullet, that's what Taylor told her. We dodged a bullet that time.

*

Tom Champion met them at the ferry dock, a squeeze, a celebration, an old family friend and then the tentative handshake for Layla. Who was she?

Tentatively welcome. Provisional. Conditional.

A drizzling black evening. She and their tiny luggage went into the backseat while Champion and Edgar talked about old friends and family matters that Layla had never heard of. Which was fine, fine. She had her secrets, too, and her surprises. It just might be yours, she thought. It *might*. Rain in slants and spatters across the black glass. Cow country all around them, green and dark, the occasional farm light through the dripping trees. The speeding sedan, the girl in the backseat, kidnapped. I am the McGuffin, she thought.

* * *

After twenty minutes or so, the lights gathered and the forest gave way and they were in a small, cute town. It was so cute. Her heart just gave out at the sight of all those picket fences, all that clapboard siding, those Norfolk Island pines and monkey-puzzle trees. Mercedes SUVs lined the sleeping streets, and tiny jaunty sports cars. No rotting snow or deer carcasses here, no derelict hot tubs, no hunting campers. Fucked, flustered and far from home. Edgar would understand that she didn't belong here, would understand why. He was from home, originally from Cut Bank. He knew which end of a chain saw was the front.

But Edgar was in the front seat, talking movie stars and Microsoft money with Tom Champion. This isn't Bigfork, Tom Champion said. This isn't the cast-iron Kokopelli crowd. These are serious collectors.

Fine with me.

They buy in depth. If they like the work, they'll take a lot of it. But they're not just buying stuff for the sake of buying. They're not on vacation.

People live here.

A lot of them, it's their second or third house. A lot of these places, you don't see the lights on too often. But, yeah, some of these people, they come and they stay, they help out with the schools, that kind of thing. Gene Hackman came to an assembly last year at my daughter's school. Nice guy, is what I hear.

* * *

Gene Hackman, Edgar said. Wow. I didn't know he was still alive.

The town itself looked like a toy, a model railroad set blown up to nearly life-size proportions, and the men's conversation seemed like it came with the town prepackaged. Men men men men manly men. Suddenly she thought of June and missed her sharply. A world without men. A prop, a love during Layla's cannibal summer. Blood and ice, bodies frozen in the streets. Daniel with his poetry and hair. It all seems miles and miles away. If men stopped going to war, would women start? It seemed like a question, anyway.

Good crowd, said Tom Champion. Through the lit front of the gallery she saw the patrons in cashmere and denim, the people from the various catalogs with their catalog haircuts and their good teeth, clutching plastic cups of wine and talk, talk, talking and twenty of the *same exact picture* on the wall. What was this?

Edgar was grinning at her, embarrassed, as he helped her out of the backseat. I didn't know, he said. I was going to tell you. . . .

And really she didn't know what there was to be nervous about and then she followed the two of them into the warm lit room and saw that they were not all the same, they were all slightly different but only slightly, and they were all drawings and paintings of her face, Layla's face. Twenty or thirty paintings of her and then the little crowd, a couple of dozen, dropped their conversations and turned toward the door where she and Edgar stood, and they smiled at her and approved and welcomed them.

* * *

A kind of panic, a feeling she didn't recognize. She backed out, knocking Tom Champion out of the way, out the door and into the rain. She couldn't breathe.

He came out after her, out into the street.

I'm sorry, Edgar said. I meant to tell you.

When, exactly? The words came to her but she couldn't get them out of her mouth, a hot ball of anger choking her, stuffed down her throat.

I thought you might like it, Edgar said. I did.

There in the road, the damp dripping all around them. The lights faded in the rain to sudden infinite black night.

My face, she finally said.

It's not, he said. That's not what this is about. Come take a look.

No.

Please.

She didn't have anything to say.

Please, he said again.

The thing was, she loved him, she did. He didn't mean her any harm. But all those pictures of her face, all those people looking at her. And she was a hardheaded girl, besides, didn't like to back down to anybody, wouldn't give an inch. But maybe she should just give in. She wasn't doing so good, doing things her way. Maybe Edgar was right or maybe she should just let herself believe that he was, just let go, let herself be led.

OK, she said. Let's have a look.

They walked in slowly as a dream. The little crowd parted, left an empty circle around them as they started around the gallery. She recognized the first one from that rainy day in the fly shop, she recognized the light, the memory of it, soft pencil gray.

This was the seed, maybe, the place where the rest of them started: that day. It all started there. From that first pencil portrait they grew and shifted shape and color, a few in crayon, a few in oils, each of them the same size, her size, maybe two feet tall and eighteen inches wide and each of them in the same silver frame, like looking into mirror after mirror: this one in bright blocky colors, the next almost a photograph. Each of them a likeness and a mood. It was like weather, the feelings shifting face-to-face, now stern, now sad, now secretly amused. She looked like she had a secret in many of them and it was strange to think that she did have a secret and it was a secret secret that not even Edgar knew, that nobody knew but her. It was strange to see her secret staring back at her out of each distorting mirror, each new version of her, looking back.

All this was fine, she supposed, a game almost. The small variations, the constant theme, it did after a while seem smart. Until the last.

* * *

At first she thought it was just a blank, a frame with black nothing in it, which seemed a clever finale. Then she saw her face emerge from the blackness, a coating of wax or crayon over the whole surface and the lines of her face emerging from deep scratches, down to the canvas. The face looked like it had been torn out of the darkness and the expression was one she recognized, she knew the feeling though she had never seen it on her own face, the sorrow torn from her, everything in loving him and not having him. The place of sorrow itself, where she touched, dead children frozen in the snow. All her dead children. How did he know this about her?

It's beautiful, she said. I hate it.

Don't say that.

I just feel . . . *naked*, you know? You set me up.

I love you, Edgar said.

Yeah, but you set me up.

Suddenly Tom Champion was there between them and they were in a room again, with people again, the bubble burst. Some people I'd like you to meet, he said to Edgar. Sorry to break in but they've been here for a while—I want you to meet them before they leave.

Taking Edgar by the elbow, leading him toward the door, leaving Layla at the back of the room with only her black mirror for company. He looked back at her, a pleading look, and she knew that nothing had really been broken, not yet. She would forgive him for now. It was bad, this thing he had done. At the same time, a little thrilling. It felt dangerous, declarative. Nobody here knew what the secret was, but everybody in the gallery that night would know there was a secret. Her secret. She looked again around the gallery, to see her own face looking back at her from every wall, in every mood and circumstance. Like the weather, she thought. I am just like the weather. Everybody talks about *me*.

*

Mexico: it could have been Morocco, anywhere.
They spread the brochures out on the dining room table—RL had
gone to Wide World of Travel especially to get them—and shoulder to shoulder they pored over the possibilities. They didn't speak
of the impossibilities. Sparkling waters, palm trees and blue skies.
Outside was sullen November night, a little above freezing, six
inches of last week's snow slowly melting only to freeze again in the
small hours of the morning.

Betsy liked the looks of Puerto Vallarta though the snorkeling
was probably better in Cabo. RL thought San Miguel de Allende
looked pretty good. Anything. Anywhere but here. The chemo was
to start up again the next day, the last round.

* * *

I'm always drunk when I see you, Betsy said. Why is that? I'm never drunk the rest of the time.

Whiskey makes me handsome and funny.

Does it work on me? she asked. Does it make me beautiful?

It does, he thought, yes, it does. But he didn't say it. The long slow curve of her neck, her hips in the hippie skirt she wore. Actually, in the small light of the dining room, the skirt looked elegant, swank even. RL had the feeling of a broken promise in her elegance. He saw her as she was now and at the same time as she had been in her twenties, nothing birdlike or nervous but slow walking and intelligent. She would consider a long moment before she would respond to something he said, she would think before she spoke, which RL found unnerving. He was never careful. Their little time together, he remembered as one blunder after another. They could never get it right, neither one of them. He would start when she was stopped and then he would stop but she would be going again except in bed. There they shut up and let it go. His dick stirred at the memory of it, the nearness of Betsy.

You don't need any help, he said. You're pretty much beautiful all the time.

Don't make me laugh, she said. Don't make me cry.

I'm not kidding.

Then the whiskey is doing its wicked work, she said.

*

June walks through the front door of her own house, and there is Howard Emerson sitting at the dining room table taking a call. Except that it doesn't feel like her own house anymore or look like it. Her own furniture, everything she's touched and stained and lived with, is in a ministorage unit out by the Wye, and Howard has moved Northern California in its place—at least what looks like Northern California—dark wood and ferns and faux Frank Lloyd Wright. Maybe it wasn't California, it was hard to say. Not Montana, anyway. Nor June.

Howard snapped his phone shut and beamed at her. Everything went great, he said.

June said, You're wearing your hat in the house again.

* * *

He blinked at her for a moment, a little angry, just a little. Then took his hat off and hung it on the chair back.

She asked, They're going to buy the place?

Why are you angry at me? he asked. I'm just trying to do what you said you wanted me to do.

I'm not angry.

That's peculiar, then, Howard said. Because you're acting exactly like you are.

I'm just unsettled, baby. I just want . . . I don't even know what I want. What happened with your clients?

June did know what she wanted, just then, which was to see him gone. But she knew, well, she didn't know anything. If the feeling was still there in a week she'd have to do something about it. For the moment she just felt tired, tired.

I don't think they're the ones, he said. They don't keep horses, and this place is really going to sell to somebody who wants the acreage, not just let it go to knapweed. But I could tell they were tempted. And they definitely have the money. Even at the price we're asking, they come out of the Seattle market and everything looks like Mexico to them. Third world.

I'm scared, she said. The words surprised her coming out of her mouth but she couldn't seem to stop.

* * *

I'm tired and I'm scared and I'm tired of taking care of myself, she said. I want you to be the man I want you to be, I want somebody to take care of me, I want—just for once—to feel safe.

She laughed, not in a pleasant way.

I don't even know what that word means, she said. *Safe.*

A falling-down time, Howard said.

What does that even mean?

I had mine in Seattle, he said. Everybody gets a falling-down time. You can't get up. You have to have somebody to help you get up.

Come to Jesus, June said.

A little bit, Howard said. A little bit of Jesus for me. Mostly it was my daughter and my ex-wife. It's a funny thing, I can't stand her now but she did save my life. And it wasn't like we were getting along all that well back then, either. We were well on our way.

I don't want to be *rescued*, she said. I'm not drowning, at least not yet.

That's the problem, Howard said. You can't be rescued until you're actually drowning. Just thinking you might drown isn't enough.

You're always telling me the way things are, she said. The way the world works. And, you know, I wish I could just believe you. I wish I could trust you. But then I think that might be letting go of things I need to hold on to, you know, like the way I need to protect myself. I can't stop protecting myself even if I wanted to.

You can trust me, Howard said. I am who I am.

But that's what I don't know, she said. Are you even kind?

I am kind of kind, he said. Kind of.

June walked out on him then, into the kitchen with the stranger's table and chairs and the stranger's art on the walls and foreign plants. She'd given up on houseplants ten years back when she killed the last of them. Poured herself a nice big glass of wine and back into the dining room, where Howard was squinting into his phone again.

I'll get myself a Coke in a minute, he said. Thanks.

I'm sorry, June said.

That's all right.

I'm just like, there's no place in this world where I belong any-more, she said. I didn't use to be homeless, I've never known what it felt like until now. Homeless.

You've got a home. As long as I've got mine.

It's not the same.

* * *

No, it isn't, Howard said. I thought that was the point, I thought you'd about had it with the same. You've had the same for twenty years. Don't get me wrong, I know. You've got that shell, and then you've got to break the shell, and it hurts.

You've got to be right even about being wrong, she said. I don't even know how to screw my life up the right way.

Sorry, Howard said.

She had managed to hurt his feelings, she could see that. Somehow this felt all right to her. But she could see that they had to change the game if they wanted to last the night. Which she did. She was so tired of being alone that Howard seemed worth her while.

Let's go out, she said. I'll buy you a Shirley Temple.

No, you won't.

No?

Not tonight, he said. Tonight you'll buy me a scotch on the rocks, if you want to go out. I'm not saying it's a good idea.

I'm a little tired of good ideas.

Let's go, then, Howard Emerson said. Let's go now.

*

Love in the whirlwind. Love in the gutter. Love in the late morning early winter when the light slants cold and gray through hospital windows. Love, he thought, of an indeterminate kind. His love—his unlikely or possible love—lay sleeping, breathing, surrounded by machines. Oh, Betsy, Beth, Elizabeth.

He kissed her sleeping hand.

*

Baby baby baby baby baby baby baby baby baby baby baby baby baby baby baby baby baby baby baby, a Thermoscan in-ear thermometer, a six-month subscription to the cloth diaper service, a new book, a Thomas the Tank Engine video and six or eight new blankets and quilts, all of them in baby baby baby blue because this time IT'S A BOY!

Edgar removes himself. The space between inside and outside is expanding, farther and farther away from himself until he feels like he might just disappear into it, this mournful . . . All women anyway except one husband, some friend of Amy's from work who hadn't gotten the message somehow that he didn't have to go to the baby shower. All clean well-scrubbed Rocky Mountain girls in the prime of life, skiers and runners and girls who fished, though not, he had to say, like Layla fished. That girl could turn a fat trout in a bathtub.

Three thirty on a winter Sunday. Hard sunlight shining on the snow in the yard, too cold to melt. Almost too bright to look at. Snowmelt dripping from the boots by the kitchen door. The smell of coffee, the memory of Layla's body stretched out the length of the bed. Breakfast in bed on the island, when she told him, the way he never quite got a look at her but just fragments and glimpses. She kept her face, her belly.

Edgar and Amy were going to have a son.

He poured a thimble of bourbon for himself and stood by the window, looking out at the hard sunlight.

Already he felt himself failing this boy. He would not allow himself. He would find a way back to Amy. She was a loving person and preoccupied with the child and the coming child and it was not a good time and Edgar reminded himself that he had loved her once. He saw the boy at ten, at thirteen, fatherless. Riding a bicycle alone through the gravel alleys. A pet, something to talk to. No clear way forward. Edgar would not allow this to happen. He carried that boy's loneliness inside him still, a thing that time could not erase, nor marriage. That was where he and Layla touched, in that lonely place, he thought. Cold blinding light outside. In all the cold world she touched him. He must not, would not pass this loneliness on.

And here was Amy, standing in the doorway. Come on, she said. Come on out. Everybody's here.

* * *

In a minute, he said.

Please.

I'll be there in a minute, Edgar said. Just give me a minute. I'll be right out.

Eggs and sausages by the side of the stove, the big cast-iron griddle waiting for huckleberry pancakes, fresh-ground coffee from the Butterfly brewed with filtered water, a big bowl of halved oranges standing by the squeezer, real maple syrup and butter from organic cows, toast and tea in case she had switched over to tea, Layla was home.

Layla was asleep upstairs and RL was busy in the kitchen, listening to mandolins and Martin Dreadnaughts at background volume, more like a little color to the air than anything else, the air that smelled of fresh coffee, the light coming flat and gray from a winter Sunday, a patchwork of ice on the ground and low gray skies. The prodigal daughter, he thought, except not prodigal. The flight the night before had been delayed and then delayed again by ice-fog, and when they finally were allowed to land and driving back to town the trees looked like white ghosts of themselves, each twig and branch encased in a skin of white ice.

Just to have her with him, under his roof, breathing the same air. He had not realized until he saw her down the jetway how lonely he had been. RL knew the drill and he was fine with it, more or less: you tied their shoes and taught them to drive and which fork to use when—he hoped he had gotten this one right—and then they up and left you. Like a dog, you bought a dog and you took care of it and you had fun with it and you let it all the way into your life and then the dog died. Kids were better. They only went away and got interested in parts of life that weren't you, which was OK in principle—otherwise he would have gotten stuck in Ohio where his parents used to be—but in practice it was no good. The only game in town, he guessed. Still it was awfully nice to have her back.

Maybe it was time to get a dog again.

Something a little bit off about the girl when he picked her up last night. She said she was exhausted, just wanted to say good night and go when they got home, something tired and tight in her face that made him believe her, some way she kept herself from him so he felt like he never got a good look at her. Elusive as ever. Maybe something else, though, maybe something more. The city taking its toll.

Ice crunched in the driveway: June's Prius, come to join them. RL felt a moment of jealousy—my house, my daughter—then remembered that he had invited them, thinking that Layla would surely be up by noon. He watched June's boyfriend unlimber himself out of the passenger seat, the white dome of his head naked to the morning. Then the hat. Howard, RL remembered. The white of Betsy's shoulder that same pale.

* * *

Black dog came running: no daughter, no Betsy, a blank place and nothing he could do about it.

But the smell of coffee roused him, and the sight of the two of them snipping and snarking in the driveway. Something pleasant about watching some other couple fight. Oh June, he thought. Beware of the hardheaded woman.

RL greeted them at the door with a shush. She's still asleep, he whispered. She got in late last night.

I was wondering, June said, with the fog and all . . .

Hot coffee, Howard said. I could really use some hot coffee.

You're in the right place, RL said, aware as he did so that Howard didn't like him any better than he liked Howard. June knew it, too, and they circled the kitchen uneasily.

Smells great in here, said Howard.

Thanks, said RL, and turned to June. So how does it feel to be rich?

I'm not rich.

Hell of a lot closer than I am.

It's depressing, isn't it? Howard said. You finally get to be a millionaire at the exact same moment when it doesn't mean a thing anymore. Every Tom, Dick and Harry.

* * *

I heard two million, RL said to June.

Two million four, Howard said.

RL wasn't actually going to poke Howard in the nose if he kept answering June's questions, but it was nice to think so.

When do you move? RL asked her.

First of the year, June said. I can't even think about it. I'm just going to pack a suitcase and live out of that for a while, put everything else in storage. Just hire somebody to do it.

Go to Hawaii.

I wish, she said. I might take a week in January, take a little break. But, no, I'm just going to work, same as usual.

Buy a new place?

Eventually, she said. Right now I'm moving into Howard's.

RL had no rights in this matter and he knew it, but still it felt like a punch in the stomach. Why? It didn't even make sense. But Howard must have seen it as he hurried to answer.

Not like living together living together, he said. Not like a couple of college students. I have a mother-in-law apartment over my garage.

It's really very nice, said June.

* * *

So she must have seen it, too, in his face.

It smells like horses, Howard said.

Not so bad, said June.

Good morning, everybody, said a sleepy Layla from the doorway.

The energy in the room recalculated itself and shifted with her emergence, little shafts of light, girlish. . . . In her pink fuzzy bathrobe Layla went from each to each and kissed them in turn, even Howard, gliding across the kitchen floor without her feet seeming to touch the ground, hidden from view beneath the pink teddy-bear fur. Here was something. What? RL made himself look away before she caught his face and saw how he loved her, how unprotected he was, naked, and a father must never be so naked. He poured a cup of coffee and tried to give it to her.

Oh, she said. No, no thanks.

Again that sense of her not quite in the room, something withheld, behind.

I've just been off the coffee lately, Layla said. Seattle, you know.

I thought Seattle was coffee world headquarters, Howard said.

That's more or less the problem, Layla said. She filled the teakettle and started it on the stove and then she turned to June. I hear you're filthy rich.

* * *

Not exactly. Closer than I used to be.

We should go buy some shoes.

There's still nowhere to buy shoes in town, June said. Unless you want to look like me.

They all looked at June's wholesome, comfortable clogs then, roundish cork-lined things of Swedish leather. Brown. All sturdy and wholesome, RL thought. They looked like June.

Layla said, I don't know why you don't come to Seattle sometime. There are ridiculous places to buy shoes there. Anything you want.

I will, June said. Though, truth be told . . .

No reason to spend that kind of money, Howard said.

This was the moment RL caught the bar smell on him, the stale breath of last night's whiskey. This was unexpected. A momentary double take and this was where Howard caught him noticing, a little glint of defiance: so what? Is this any of your business?

In my house, RL said, when a beautiful woman wants to buy some shoes, we just stand back and get out of the way.

June laughed out loud and Howard glared at her, then at RL.

Howard said, Three hundred dollars for a pair of shoes.

* * *

I've spent that on a pair of Tony Lamas, RL said. Probably shouldn't have but I did.

He smiled, pleased with himself, then looked at his daughter to see if she was pleased with him, too. But Layla was clouding up, somewhere off inside and unhappy.

You OK, baby?

Layla held up a hand, a stop sign, palm out—half covered her face with her other hand—then turned, and bolted from the room. They all stood silent for a moment, each of them looking from face to face and then back at the empty place where the girl had been. Then June said, I'll go take a look, if that's OK.

Fine with me, said RL.

I'm going to go run a couple of errands, Howard said. Just while I'm in town. I've got the cell.

And everybody left, and there was RL all by himself again, in his kitchen full of loveless food, the middle of the morning, the middle of the winter, the late middle of his life. Sparkle and fade, RL thought. What the hell was wrong with his girl? He went to the window and looked out at the rotten patchwork of snow in his yard and thought of Mexico. The beach, he thought. Somewhere with sun and palm trees, some temporary respite. A day. A week. It was impossible to say.

*

June on her knees, the perfumed many-colored twilight of the old church, the beads of the rosary between her clumsy fingers. Holy Mary, mother of God, forgive me, she thought. I was apparently mistaken.

The smell of myrrh.

She had become a woman without a home. She had become a woman without a story. She had become a woman who prayed the rosary alone in church on a Sunday afternoon while Howard bet on football games and drank red beer at the Paradise Falls casino. She kept secrets from everybody and everybody kept secrets from her.

But mainly she had become unreal. If she held her hand up to the rose window, she could see right through it, the stained-glass shepherds and their crooks and sheep. She knelt so lightly as to be made from light itself, from oxygen and helium, from thought. When Rosco died, she lost the last thing connecting her to the world and now she thought bitterly of herself and how lightly she held his life. An old dog spindle-shanked and water eyed. Once they had been sleek and fast, both of them. Then at the end she had talked— to RL, to Layla—as if it didn't matter, as if it was something to be taken lightly, a joke almost. True, he was a dog and dogs didn't over-hear, but June had heard herself and remembered. Dogs and money, money and love, love and alcohol, alcohol and death, death and dogs, she felt her thoughts spinning round and round and tried to center herself again on the simple fact of the beads between her fingers, the dim light and perfumed quiet: *Holy Mary, mother of God . . .*

Because, she thought, alcohol is death. That need for annihila-tion, no stranger to herself. Annihilation at the end of every road: at the end of time, the bottom of the bottle, the deep and dreamless sleep she remembers from her childhood. She doesn't sleep like that anymore but dreams and shakes and tumbles from one side of the bed to the other. Last night it was a wedding, her own wedding but not the one to Taylor, some other man, she never even saw his face . . . Layla had been at the dream wedding, with her baby, a baby girl, a little pink flower.

Return to center, June thought. A bat shriek of sexuality inaudi-ble to any but herself. It echoes in the old church, slowly fills the corners, like water. Drown, she thought. The baby they never got around to and then it was too late. Take that life and give it to the baby, drown in baby love, *the fruit of thy womb*. . . . Dogs and money, money and love, love and alcohol, alcohol and death, death and dogs, dogs and babies, the whirling world around her and nothing to stop June from spinning along with it, the whirlwind.

RL *looked for her in the darkness* before dawn, the airport lit and busy while the moon set slowly behind the mountains to the north, a lip of bright reflection outlining the peaks and saddles. Above, the night sky still full of stars, clear, cold and bright.

Taxis, wives and boyfriends, late-season hunters with their rifle cases and coolers full of elk meat, a hotel shuttle dropping off the crew, everybody a little off under that big black sky, a little sad or sleepy or just unnaturally clean, like a face on the TV with the brightness turned up too high. He watched for her little Toyota, half expecting her to skip it. She'd park in long-term parking anyway. It was cheaper. RL felt restless as a bride.

* * *

A dog-faced man in a leather jacket came out in a breath of warm airport-scented air, lit a cigarette a foot from RL's face and swore at the morning.

I wouldn't go to Memphis if I didn't have to, he said. You know that.

It took RL a moment to realize that he had an earpiece, a cell phone and not a regular walkie-talkie crazy man like the one down by the Food Farm.

We can talk about her when I get back, he said. The money, it's none of your business. It's not the problem.

RL could hear the angry bee voice in the man's earhole, a female bee.

I told you, he said. She's just a thing—we can talk about her later. Look, I've got to board now, they're boarding the flight. I'll call you tonight. No, I love you, too, I just have to run.

He slapped his tiny phone shut with an emphatic flick of the wrist and grinned at RL. The lie hung in the air in the white of his breath.

Not even seven in the morning, he said to RL.

RL shrugged: what are you going to do? Now the lie was his, too.

Six forty-five in the morning and she's up and bitching me out.

* * *

I don't know, RL said.

Beautiful girl, though, said the dog-faced man, fishing the ear-piece out of his earhole and examining it for wax. Still makes my dick hard to look at her.

He stubbed his cigarette out and wandered back inside, apparently humming to himself. When RL turned back toward the parking lot, Betsy was there.

Who was that? she asked.

Face like an unmade bed, bags falling from her every side, a dim profusion of color and stripes and paisley green. She was ready to turn and bolt right then and there and RL wondered, not for the first time, if this was such a hot idea.

Nobody I know, he said, but he sounded like he was lying.

She grinned at him disbelieving and pecked his cheek and said, Off to Mexico!

RL followed her through the automatic doors and into the warm chemical air, wondering at her many bags and baskets, the giant Rollaboard that trailed behind her, feeling smallish and tight with his tiny bag and his prim little carry-on. Nevertheless he was equipped: sun-blocking shirts and a giant hat and special fingerless gloves and a twelve-weight Sage rod with a reel the size of a Big Ben alarm clock. This last seemed like a ridiculous thing, but he had been warned not to go light. In his mind's eye RL saw himself casting into sunny sky-blue water. He knew himself for a fool. He could easily rent the gear in Mexico, if he had the time at all to fish. It seemed possible that it would all get safely back to Montana unused, the rod, the reel, the brand-new line. But it was like touching the thing itself was the same as fishing in bright blue water. Like buying the thing was the same as having the experience. This was how RL made a good part of his living, selling fancy stuff to doctors and executives to take back to New Jersey with them, to shove back into the office closet for another year and touch once in a while to remind them of autumn days on the Missouri or a blue-wing olive hatch where the twenty inchers couldn't stop themselves. That fine English reel, that Tom Morgan rod with their name imprinted just above the reel seat. He knew them for fools but he was no different. No different.

I've been up since three, she said. I didn't sleep at all last night.

You can sleep on the plane, he said.

Or I can drink myself silly, she said.

Edgar ran the river path in the dawn light, the trash and alders by the waterside in and out of the fog, the river itself coming and going and strangely a few risers out in the safe middle of the channel. Most rivers, the big fish stayed to the edges and left the main channel for dinks and suckers, but here the big boys swam in the heavy current, the water thick with winter cold, the ice lacing the slow water by the bank. The air was cold with tiny crystals of ice suspended in it so it hurt his lungs to breathe it. Which was fine with Edgar. He pushed himself faster.

His nose dripped snot and his head hurt. He had overdressed himself in wool and now his back and belly prickled with sweat, last night's last shot tracing its way down his cheek in a drip of frozen poison. He took his wool cap off and stuffed it in his pocket and the cold burned his naked ears. His calves burned and his eyes teared up. Still, he went faster, pushed harder.

He knew she was home, knew RL had flown off to Mexico that morning. Still he wasn't going to go there.

Cars swished by on the bridge overhead, making so much more noise than they knew they were making, tires on wet pavement. Everything melting or still frozen. Lamps in windows looking yellow and warm in this first light of morning. The night so long this time of year. Night so long and the Hellgate wind so cold it blew right through his bones. He had a scrap of folk song running through his head around and around: *in the pines, in the pines, where the sun never shines. . . .* He felt himself like something old, with banjos. It's a hard way to find out that trouble is real.

It's nothing new, can be said about dirt.

All these sane and reasonable lives unfolding around him, all this predictable newspaper-reading and lunch-making and child-kissing-good-bye. Toasting and percolating. Somewhere in this city a sleepy husband and a sleepy wife were making love, half awake, slow and quiet and under the covers so as not to wake the baby. It was a love world, all around him. Edgar was moving through it cold and alone, but he wasn't meant to be. Love shone down on all of it, and just now was like a winter night, long and cold but that didn't mean it wouldn't end. The sun would rise again, it always did. He was just turned sideways to it was all. The love world all around him.

Just the thought of Layla brought a small rising happiness, a warmth inside the cold shell of himself; and then the cold again, the cold fact that he must not and would not, the thought of his daughter, the son on the way . . . He had made his commitments and now was the time to be a man about them. And then, to be a man, fine, a little dead inside but holding on, holding up his end, his Amy would smile at him sometimes and wasn't that enough? It ought to be enough. It would have to be enough.

In another lifetime it would be enough. In another skin.

He knocked and held his breath, listening for footsteps, which he did not hear. She was asleep or gone. The world, which had seemed brightly colored and dangerous a moment before, now resumed its gray face. Snow rotting in the dead grass.

Then silently the door cracked open and she was there in her bathrobe, sleep all in her face. She looked surprised, worried. She didn't open the door any further.

Can I come in? he asked.

She had to think about it.

I thought you weren't going to come around anymore, she said. I thought we were done with this.

I was just out for a run.

I can see that, she said; and just then he turned inside out and saw himself as she must have seen him, wounded and sweaty, begging on her doorstep in a dirty sweatshirt.

I didn't mean to bother you, he said. I'll just, uh.

* * *

You might as well, she said, and swung the door open.

He entered unembraced or kissed and sat down at the kitchen table. She said, I'm going to make some coffee, and then started making coffee. She said, I've been having crazy dreams. Last night I was dancing the mambo with this guy I knew from my first year of school, my poetry TA. I don't even know what the mambo is supposed to look like but there I was dancing it.

I love you, he said.

I know you do. That's not exactly the issue, is it?

It's like you're enjoying this.

No, she said, and turned the coffeemaker on, and sat down across the table from him as it began to gurgle and hiss. No, I'm not enjoying this at all. I'm the opposite of enjoying this.

I should go.

No, you should.

Neither one of them moved. It started to rain or hail outside, a soft patter on the window glass.

RL is down in Puerto Vallarta, Edgar said.

RL has lost his mind, Layla said. There seems to be some of that going around lately, the crazy bug. I got bit with the crazy bug last week when you didn't call and you wouldn't answer an e-mail or anything.

I'm sorry, he said.

I just sort of went a little crazy around the house, she said. At least I didn't go flying off to Mexico with my ex-girlfriend from a hundred and fifty years ago.

What's the deal with her?

I have no idea, Layla said. Not a fucking clue. You could ask my dad when he gets back, but I don't think he has any better idea. Just restless, is my bet. Crazy bug bit him.

She gave him a tight false smile and Edgar had never seen a person so unhappy as she. And he made her so. This was his doing. He could think of nothing more to say.

He'll get over it, Layla said. He always does.

As if nothing mattered, as if it were all illusion, the hope and pain together. A game they couldn't stop playing but no more consequential. This bitterness. She was too young to feel this, too lovely. Edgar remembered her as he had drawn her, that lovely stillness in her eyes. She knew more than he did, she *understood*. A thing he loved about her. Now she didn't understand anything, she just saw through things.

She got up, poured coffee, gave him his cup and sat down again. Morning light, her hand curled around the coffee cup.

* * *

I've been having crazy dreams myself, he said. Last night I was trying to cut this tree down with a chain saw, a big fir tree with limbs all the way down to the ground. I had to cut my way into it to even get to the trunk, and then every time I made a cut, it started to lean toward the house like it was going to fall on it and so I had to stop and start again on the other side.

Whose house?

It was my house, Edgar said, I think. But there was nobody in it. I don't know how I knew that, but it felt like there was nobody home.

None of this was true. Edgar never remembered his dreams. But he had the feeling that if he kept talking, he could keep her in the room, keep her with him. Her hand opened from her coffee cup and rested on the table.

He said, Every time I went to the other side of the tree, though, when I started to cut, it leaned in that direction and there was the house!

Like magic, she said.

Oh, he said. Just the rules are different over on the other side.

The other side of what?

Didn't you ever think that? That whole other world over on the other side? Just as real as this one, and we're just the dream that they're having over on the other side. We just don't remember it right. They wake up over on the other side and they say to each other, I had the most amazing dream.

You were alone a lot, weren't you? When you were little.

I was a complicated kid, Edgar said.

Were you happy?

I don't know, he said. Happy enough. I had friends, some of them not even imaginary.

Her hand opened on the table between them. All he had to do was take it.

RL showed me some pictures of you a while back, he said. You in your little birthday crown. Big old stuffed pink pig. Bigger than you.

Pork Chop, Layla said. He's up in my closet right now.

You were beautiful.

Layla laughed, unhappy.

Everybody's beautiful when you're a kid, she said. Everybody's got that perfect skin and that beautiful hair, everybody's slim and pretty and talking to the angels all day. People don't get older. They just get worse.

It's not true, you know.

* * *

What part?

Plenty of fat kids out there.

Not you.

No, he said. I was the one whose ears stuck out. My teeth were crooked and I was so skinny that I looked like a zipper. My teachers thought I was smart.

I bet you were cute, she said.

He took her hand then, and they looked at them, their hands clasped together on the tabletop, as if they were independent animals, unattached, little comfort-seeking comfort-loving animals with an instinct for each other. The tap of rain or hail against the window. Then they were standing, kissing, and Layla was just as tall as he was but soft, pretty, pliant, a hardheaded girl but soft everywhere else and a feeling of surrender, of weightlessness, that moment on the Gravitron when you're just spinning, spinning with nothing but air below your feet, kissing, and then they were in her bedroom, surrounded by her childhood, and then they were naked on her childhood bed and he was inside her and she was weeping but she did not want him to stop. Would not let him stop. Tears and snot all on his neck and, yes, there was something hot about it, something deep, something he didn't want to think about but did not let himself think but just gave up, let go, deep inside her.

*

Howard, drunk, and June, drunk, and the record player was also drunk. He kept on trying to play an old LP of George Jones, but it always stuck at the same place and wouldn't go any further: *the lip-print on a half-filled cup of coffee that you poured and didn't drink, poured and didn't drink, poured and didn't drink . . .*

The CD is a fraud and conspiracy, Howard said. He took the record elaborately from the turntable and sprayed it with a special spray and wiped it with a special blue cloth and set it back on the platter with the careful movements of the experienced drunk.

The music is still on there with a CD, but it's like a curtain or something, he said. Like a veil. But with one of these, the music is just there, it's printed on there, the music itself.

* * *

As I have said repeatedly, June said, I believe you.

Get everybody to buy the same exact music over and over again, Howard said. Next thing you know, it'll be the microdigital whosi-whatsis with the curb feelers and the mud flaps.

George Jones sang, *There goes my reason for living.* A gloom of alcoholic regret hung in the semidarkness, or maybe it was too early for regret, maybe it was pre-regret, drinking and smoking and knowing that none of this would seem like a good idea in the morning. June poured herself another little glass of wine and Howard puffed at his big cigar. None of it mattered anyway. This amber melancholy. It fit her like an old sweater, like something she had worn everyday once but couldn't bear to throw out, though the whiskey-colored wool was frayed and tattered.

The inside of Howard's house, she thought, was like the inside of Howard's brain, dark and cluttered with Western memorabilia, an elk's head over the fireplace, a pony-skin rug tossed over the back of the sofa, much evidence of killing. The room itself was cheaply made of modern materials and the fireplace ran unflickering on gas. The room did not end in the corners but just trailed off into indefinite darkness. Pictures of horses, paintings of buffalo against a winter backdrop, hooves breaking through the snow to find the meager grass beneath. As if, she thought. Put either one of us out in that and we'd freeze solid in an afternoon.

I wish, she said.

I want to go back out to Seattle one of these days, he said. I'm getting too old for the winters.

* * *

I thought you hated Seattle.

I do, he said. Don't get me wrong. That city is a first-class shit-hole, pardon my French.

Then why do you want to go there?

Who said I wanted to go there?

You did.

I'm just tired of the winters is all. Maybe we should head down to Tucson after Christmas. San Diego, someplace.

I have to work, remember?

No, you don't. I'm the one that has to work. You're the one with all the money in the world. Plus there's the horses to take care of. Who's going to feed the horses if we're off on a golf course some-where?

I don't golf, she said. But she said it just to have something to do with her mouth, to help her to breathe, keep breathing because she had seen that he was angry with her. Something black and bitter and real was alight in him. And June had done him no wrong.

Through the fog of alcohol she saw that she had done him no wrong and he was angry with her.

What's the matter? Howard said.

Oh, June said, trying to breathe, nothing. I think I left my phone in the other house.

What do you need a phone for?

Alcohol is making a fool of you, she thought, but she did not say so. Instead, she launched herself out of the depths of his leather chair and up and into her coat in one motion and through the kitchen and out the back door where little starving deer stopped moving at the sight of her. They stood absolutely still at the edge of the yard light where they gathered every night. They were scared of June. The storm door shut behind her with a sigh and she was all the way outside, maybe ten degrees and clear, all the way to Mars.

The cold air sobered her up in an instant. The boozy layer of warmth and goo was gone and she stood naked to herself. Fool that I am, she thought.

Because there were only a few reasons to be angry with somebody, in her experience. Either she had given Howard offense, which she had not, or he was jealous of her, which he had no reason to be—Howard with the home, now, the power, the say. Which left one possibility, which was that he was angry because he had done her wrong.

Another human paradox, she thought. Built crossways and deranged. You hurt somebody and then you've just got to get mad at them because you can't let things be right between you because they aren't right because you hurt them. What on earth had Howard done to her?

* * *

204

Something.

The hungry deer stared at her from the edge of the light, too nervous to graze, too hungry to run. She thought with a sudden longing of Dorris MacKintyre and his oxygen tank, just an ordinary buzzard without a plan for anyone. Suffering had made him holy, she thought. Maybe it would work for her. He had not started as a perfect man—you could see it in his daughter's face sometimes, that flash of fear, that final tiny unwillingness to trust completely after all these years. And yet the Dorris she knew was better than anybody, light and clean and willing to be happy on the smallest excuse. Suffering had polished him bright.

Not me, she thought. The mess and muck, the yard sale inside her, drunk, sober, sad, angry, loving and loveless, lonely. Fuck Howard, she thought, fuck him completely. And the rest of them, too, everybody but Layla. She laughed at herself, a small and stupid person, homeless. All these big plans for herself and now what? There was no way she could go back inside, not back into Howard's brain. And there was nowhere else to go but the little apartment over the garage that was, in theory, hers, but felt like a public place, a waiting room.

Salle d'attente. Anywhere but here. She wanted to be lonely among strangers instead of lonely at home, surrounded by good coffee and strange cars, hard consonants, almond pastries.

She went inside, into the mother-in-law apartment, and was instantly drunk again in the heat. All the internal structures of her brain turned into jelly and she poured herself a glass of cold water and dissolved like jelly in the water. This longing, just wanting to be clean. The river called to her. Water flowing under ice, the little dipper birds that went all the way under. They always made it out the other side, although, she thought, probably not always. That one miscalculation and they would come up where the ice was a solid sheet and drown trying to come up through it. Little tiny frozen dead bird under the ice, saddest thing in the whole round world.

The river smoking in the cold night air. Just clean.

Then Howard started banging on the door. You in there? he shouted. Where'd you go?

Bang bang bang.

Bang bang bang.

I'm here, she said.

Let me in, he said.

I don't think so.

Why not? What's the matter?

Nothing's the matter, she said. I'm drunk, it's late, I just want to go to bed. You're drunk, too.

He tried the door again and it was still locked. She felt like she ought to be scared but she wasn't. She was scared but in an almost pleasurable way, as if she were alive, outside in the cold night, running with the deer. She was dead to the world outside herself and that world was dead to her, she saw this now. This was the problem.

She went to her purse and took out her key ring with its small attached can of pepper spray. It said in big red letters that it was only to be used on wildlife and that it was a violation of federal law to use this product in a manner inconsistent with its labeling.

Howard, she said through the door. Howard, are you listening?

He said nothing but tried the door again, which was still locked tight.

Howard, I'm going to bed, she said. I'm going to sleep. We can talk in the morning.

I don't know what's wrong.

What's wrong is that you're trying to break down my door in the middle of the night, June said. She felt lovely and lucid and calm.

Everything was fine a minute ago, he said.

No, you're right, you're absolutely right. And now it's time for bed.

Howard tried the door again halfheartedly. June thought: I will huff and puff and I will blow your house down. Then heard his footsteps on the stairway down, retreating. Good night, Howard, she thought to herself. Good night and good-bye.

Then he was gone and she was alone.

The swim-up bar was three-deep in Mormon girls ordering Virgin Marys, Arnold Palmers, Cinderellas and coco coladas. Not girls, not exactly—probably in their late twenties, early thirties, and all of them talked about their kids—but they were all as slim and pretty and blond as sorority girls and they had on two-piece bathing suits, in some cases absurdly small, and the same high birdlike twitter as sorority girls when they were in a mass together. RL sat half submerged on a barstool like three hundred pounds of half-rotten meat. Right in the middle of the Mormon girls. He was enjoying himself.

Betsy lay facedown at the side of the pool in the lively shade of the palm fronds, restless in the wind. She was swathed from hat to aqua socks in cotton and nylon, not an inch of skin exposed except her face and fingers. The rest of her hands were cased in flesh-colored fingerless gloves which RL found infinitely creepy.

Betsy had gotten, her word, *blitzed* on the airplane down and had wept herself to sleep the night before and awakened ghostly and funereal. Through breakfast she had seemed always almost with something to say, on the tip of her tongue, but she never said it. This trip had been a mistake, then. She would not be jollied along or talked out of herself. RL was already planning his alternate week: drinking one day, fishing the next, perhaps a snorkeling expedition.

The Mormon girls were decorative. RL understood that the good skin and cleavage and orthodontia were meant for the husbands in their lives, that as much as they smiled and laughed, they were not in any sense ready to party. RL was not sure he was ready to *party* himself. But all these girls, they looked like they did enjoy a good hearty heterosexual fuck once in a while, an uncomplicated few minutes in the missionary position, maybe a quickie in the shower while the baby was napping. . . . RL felt a sharp nostalgia for those days, domesticated love, nothing exotic about it, no drama, no danger. Plus, it had been a while. And it looked like it would be a while longer. It was his own fault, fat and sad, drooping over a barstool in a wet shirt, a fishing shirt with many, many pockets and loops—what right-thinking girl would want to fuck him? But he wondered if this was just another symptom of his age, this feeling that everybody else in the entire world was having sex, everybody but him. Even June was having sex, he was pretty sure. June in her comfortable shoes and practical haircut.

The next time he looked over at Betsy, she was looking back at him, or at least pointing her big black sunglasses at him. The wind rustled the fronds of the palm trees overhead, ruffling the shade, and a jet contrail drew a white line across the empty sky. Some perfect loneliness in the hard sunlight. The Mormon girls were talking about what kind of bedding they liked the best and how poor and scratchy the Mexican sheets were.

He should have figured some of this stuff out by now. It just all felt like scatter, unwilling or unable to make sense of itself. Life's rich banquet, a cornucopia of silver and shit, oranges and car parts, a French encyclopedia under a gold cup of teeth. Scatter. The Mormon girls in their little womb of money and prettiness and not even knowing they were in the womb while Mexican girls scoured plates in the back of the restaurant and women elsewhere died in childbirth without complaint. All this in a moment of blur. His own life he had spent on triviality except for his daughter. Now he was here, in a place he didn't belong, with a woman he didn't know.

She was waiting for him.

She could wait for a little while. She could stand to.

But she would not.

I'm never drinking again, she said. She looked cold in the water, which wasn't possible, the water warm as blood and the air heavy and hot. Someplace inside she was always cold.

RL tipped his piña colada in her direction. You'll be OK by sundown, he said. I always am.

I am not you, Betsy said. I feel like I'm going to fall down.

* * *

Maybe take a nap.

Walk me up to the room, she said. Would you?

She had this quality, he had noticed it before, that when she spoke to him, everybody and everything else just disappeared, just the two of them and a blur outside. Her energy field.

Let me finish this up, he said, drinking his drink.

No hurry, she said intently.

The Mormon girls had fallen silent with her approach and were now starting to chatter again, edging away, talking about whether it was safe to eat the fruit ices that they sold by the side of the road. The dark-haired one in the tiny purple two-piece, the only interesting face, had taken a chance on a skewer of shrimp, last time they were down, and paid for it the next three days. They laughed and moved away and took their laughter with them. Betsy reached out and touched RL through the wet fabric of his shirt and he felt her cold run into him.

I've got to go, she said, and when he looked into her little gray face, he saw that she was telling the whole truth. He set his drink down, left the sex and sunshine outside, helped her up the breezy stairs and into the semidarkness of her room.

Betsy sat down on the edge of her bed and said, Don't go.

The bed was still unmade from the night before, a glass of water on the bedside table, a dozen pill bottles.

* * *

I feel like I could have thought this through, she said. Just a little better.

There's nothing to worry about, RL said.

All this way, and all this money.

I've got the money, RL said. I told you. It was just something I wanted to do. It's nothing you need to worry yourself about. Take a nap, we'll go for a swim, lay around on the beach for a while. It's just something for you to enjoy.

I'm not even in my body anymore, she said. It's like I'm not even connected to it.

I can certainly see that.

It feels like Purgatory, Betsy said. It feels like Purgatory already.

Take a little nap, he said. You'll feel better.

I said good-bye to them, Betsy said.

RL felt the chill again, a cold breeze in a hot room. He went to the window and there was the Pacific, blue as an eye, stretching into haze under a few white aimless clouds.

Said good-bye to who?

Roy, she said. Roy and Ann and Adam. I didn't really say anything to the kids.

* * *

What did you tell Roy?

The same thing the oncologist told me. That last round, it worked but it didn't work well enough. He told me they just really had to hit it out of the park and they didn't, quite. Then he gave me some life advice. It was all pretty low-key. I was really calm, I was proud of myself.

I thought you weren't going to go in again till after the holidays, RL said. This was the imaging?

Oh, she said, mistake.

What kind of mistake?

I was going to go in, get the OK, she said. I had such a positive mental attitude! I was sure he was going to tell me everything was fine. I was sure of it. Then, you know, come down here with you, have a drink or two, have a little fun. It's been a while since I was really fun. I know that's what you wanted for me.

I'm sorry, he said.

What have you got to be sorry for? You're trying to do a nice thing and I appreciate it.

I wanted something else for you.

Oh, she said. No more than I did.

There seemed to be nothing more to say. He floated between the bed and the window, uncertain, unattached. It was dazzling sunlight outside the window but here in the twilight her face was a blur. A long way for a short ride, he thought. Your applause is the only paycheck that cowboy is going to cash today.

Come, she said briskly. Sit.

She patted the bed next to where she lay. RL went reluctantly. He didn't know where he was, where he was supposed to be.

Tell me what you want to do, she said.

You know.

I do, she said. But it's too late.

*

In this dream there was a baby but there was something wrong with the baby, you could tell it wasn't a real baby, it was
like a rubber baby that bleated when she squeezed it but it was a real
baby, too, and it was her baby, hers to take care of it and Layla tried,
she fed it and changed it even though there was nothing there in the
diaper, just a smooth flesh-colored mound of nothing like Barbie or
Ken; and when she held the baby to her chest to comfort it, the
baby opened its mouth and out came the sound of an electric bell
like a fire drill, insistent. It was Edgar's baby, she knew it all at once.
It was the doorbell.

It was the doorbell five in the morning and there outside the
door was June. Suitcase in her hand.

Her body in the afternoon half-light lay dim and pretty across the rumpled sheet. The room was hot and damp with sunlight creeping through the thick drapes and the windows open. She might have been asleep.

RL sat against the pillows with nothing to do. He would have lit a cigar but it would bother her. Besides, the cigars were in his own room next door along with the gin. Also, it was not yet three in the afternoon. Certainly he was on vacation but there were limits. Maybe.

She wore a black tank top and a bra, nothing else. A fake breast inside the bra, and a real one. RL did not know which was which.

* * *

She was asleep, the kind of sleep that was like falling down a well, her breathing deep and slow and somewhere clogged.

He didn't feel the way he thought he would.

He didn't see the point of Mexico anymore.

She looked beautiful. She did. Long and slim. The bone cage of her hips. Her skin all red and rough from weather was softened by the light, by the light perfumed sweat on her. In sleep she was worried still—he could see it in her face—but slipping away, falling into nothing.

Did she even want to?

She was wearing perfume. It wasn't like her. He hadn't noticed until now, or at least the front of his brain hadn't noticed. Somewhere back in the reptile brain he knew her, caught the wild scent of something sweet and fruitful. He wondered sometimes how much of his life was his and how much instinct or smell, which he thought were the same thing. Something about her he wanted. He didn't even have to know why. Something about her that didn't want him. Not enough.

He thought about her kids, faces in the rain.

He thought about Thailand: what she said, about letting the seed in, the start of something that only takes shape later on. Maybe he let the illness into himself. Maybe he opened himself up to it. The bug.

* * *

Maybe he would live long enough for it to make a difference.

Pick your poison.

Oh, he thought, oh. Something being shed. RL felt it dropping away from him without knowing what it was.

He left her then, left her sleeping, only for a moment, slipping silent as a robber into his fat man shorts and many-pocketed shirt—a ridiculous man, he knew it—across the cool tile floor and out into the hallway and next door, where he poured himself a glass of gin on ice and brought a Cuban Romeo y Julieta back to light. Giving way, letting go. What was it? He felt strange to himself.

Out on the balcony, the bluest ocean.

Never odd or even, RL thought. He lit the big cigar and watched the children in the surf. The air was hot and still and the water just cool enough so there was no reason to get out, the waves low and playful, surprised shrieks from the little girls as the water overtook them from behind, their backs to the deep blue sea and their eyes on their mommies. . . . He felt—what?—light, the dancing bear.

Oh, sad and lonely dancing bear. Oh, lonely me, he thought.

But he didn't feel it. He felt pretty good, actually. Strangely light and airy. Untethered. He had this past, this history, she had dumped him once and broken his heart, he had chosen to stay in the valley instead of testing himself in the wide world, mistakes had been made, entrances and exits blown, but even this was not all dead dogs and bad road trips. He had emerged from the past with this beautiful daughter, with the October mornings and kingfishers and the heft, the surprise of a big fish on the line. And, yes, she might be dead soon. Death was waiting for all of them. This did not seem like an excuse to not live.

Between past and future he sat, smoking and alive. Real Cubans, RL thought. As good as they say.

Thank you, God of nothing. Nobody that he used to be, nobody that he might become, no million dollars, no mending fences. His mother was still dead and he would never tell her how he loved her and he would never go to the Olympics and the person who wanted these things, he temporarily was not. He did not want to be rich or beautiful. Even Layla, beautiful as she was, he knew she was out there and for once he could rest secure and know that whatever waited for him was out there, waiting.

RL felt that he was touching something. The stream going by and him letting it. Floating in it.

Something.

He thought he would solve something by sleeping with her. He understood that now. He thought he would redress or at least reopen, but the past stayed exactly where it was, unchanged, all the old impulses and regrets, this mistaken words and the wrong silences. . . . It didn't matter now. He was here now and it was all right. There would be a future, he understood that, and something would happen in it. But for now.

* * *

Now he sat on the tiled balcony, smoking his big cigar, watching the smoke drift out into the still afternoon air. The ocean below and the sound of the wind in the palms, a restless afternoon breeze. Now it would always be four o'clock. Now an unaccustomed quiet. Now the touch, the sip, the sea breeze on his skin. Now the sailor, home from the sea. A restless rest, here. Now.

*

OK, Layla said. Now what?

June just looked at her as every single thought flew out of her head. She felt a muddy mess inside, and then suddenly she was crying, remembering Taylor, the empty womb she carried in her belly still. They tried and tried, Now here . . .

Layla saw the tears and came to comfort her but she was no comfort, crying herself.

I'm sorry, June said. I'm so sorry.

Sorry for what? Don't be.

Fuck, fuck, fuck, said June.

* * *

Layla held her at arm's length and laughed at her, still weeping.

Listen to you.

Fuck, said June.

Then they were both laughing and tears and snot ran down into each other's sweaters and it was just stupid. But good. June felt like it was good, holding Layla, there in the kitchen. June wanted it to be simple comfort but she was complicated herself, couldn't stop being herself, the barren . . . Now this girl, an easy accident, a baby.

What am I going to do? Layla asked. Tell me.

No, June said. Nobody's going to tell you.

But I don't know what to do.

And everybody else does, everybody's got an opinion. I mean, I do, too. Because it's an easy choice for me to make. It's harder for you.

I haven't told anybody else.

Nobody?

Nobody at all. Just you.

Not . . . ?

Nobody but you.

* * *

Oh, June said.

I know.

June got up, put her hand on the counter, looked out the window, touched a coffee cup where it sat dirty next to the sink. She felt like an actress on a stage, looking for some bit of business that would express her confusion and grief. What would such a person do? All fluttery and wan. All Sarah Bernhardt. Save me!

What shall we do? she asked. What shall we do?

Let's go out for breakfast, Layla said.

June considered this for a long moment. Then she said, I can't see how that will solve anything.

I didn't think it would, Layla said. Not for a moment. I could use some flapjacks, though.

True, June said.

Some eggs and taters.

Ruby's or the truck stop?

Hell, let's go all the way. Let's take the pickup, hit the truck stop, drive around for a while after, you want to? Maybe go up to the bison range, look at some buffalo. Go drink and drive.

Monkey time, June said.

* * *

What?

No drinking, June said. Not while you're . . .

One won't hurt anything.

It's nine thirty in the morning.

I'm not talking about now. I'm talking about later. Maybe we can go up to Hot Springs, up to the Symes. I could stand to warm up for once.

We'll see, June said.

One won't hurt anything.

We'll see, June said.

*

Her name was April, he was almost sure, and he met her at that party in Madrona—he remembered the house, the Richie Rich club, a bunch of California boys with a hot tub and a view of Lake Washington . . . and they had made it back here somehow, and now she was sleeping the sleep of the undead but not quite snoring with her eye makeup, much eye makeup, smeared across Daniel's pretty pillowcase. Sunday morning, a low slant of light. It was time to change his life.

*

The thing is, Layla said, I know this is supposed to be bad news and all. I know this is trouble. But part of me, down in my body, part of me is happy. My body is fucking thrilled about this. You know?

I don't know, June said.

I'm sorry.

No, June said, I didn't mean it like that.

They drove in RL's big pickup, Layla behind the wheel, across the reservation on patched and rutted two-lane. A mixed winter sky of black and brilliant blue raced by overhead, promising sunshine, promising snow. A black-and-white cow in a field, a rusting Farmall, a solitary pine tree with its shadow outlined in ice. Not another car in sight, and the only house on the far corner of the hayfield, nestled in among windbreak cedars at the base of the hill. They were the lucky ones, the only ones to see it, all this ordinary beauty.

It's strange, June said, how much you just sort of get what you get.

Layla burst out laughing. She said, What the hell was that?

June surfaced out of her thoughts, surprised a little at herself.

Sorry, she said. Just the tail end of a long conversation with my brain.

And what did you have to say to yourself?

Well, I was thinking.

What?

Oh, I don't mean to put you on the spot or anything. But I was thinking about you, what you ought to do, whether I should try to tell you to do something. I don't mean anything by that, it's just, is there anything I could do to help?

No, I get it.

Good, June said. And then it was like, how much of my life is going after something and then getting it and then how much is just like something happens and there you are.

* * *

So you think I should keep the baby.

I didn't say that.

So you don't think I should keep the baby.

I didn't say that either. You think it's a baby?

What?

You think of it as a baby, and not some thing down inside of you. Some lump.

No, it's definitely a baby. The other night I had a dream where I could see her face. I've been having crazy complicated dreams lately.

Well, June said. That's something.

What kind of something?

I don't know.

No, tell me.

June waited as they came down a long curving hill to meet the other highway where it came up out of the river valley, gray fields and black crows under a sky that was suddenly covered in black cloud. Crows circling over the highway. It seemed like a day when all bets were off, all regular life suspended. June reached into the cooler behind the seat and brought out a cold dripping can of beer and opened it. Layla had packed the cooler but not for herself.

* * *

I think you're going to have a baby, June said, that's what I think.

Oh, me, too, said Layla. A girl baby.

You don't have to.

Oh, yes, I do, Layla said. That other stuff, that's fine for other people, you know? I'm not making any judgment about it or anything. But I've been thinking and I just don't think it's for me.

Abortion, you mean, June said. She was suddenly tired of this fog of romance, this inspecificity. You're going to keep the baby.

I don't know what I'm going to do with the baby, Layla said.

But you're going to carry it to term.

Yes, I am, Layla said. She swiped the beer out of June's hand and took a short sip and it started to snow, a brief furious assault. Layla turned the wipers on and strained through the windshield to see the road, a momentary whiteout, the big truck floating in space. June watched terrified.

They drove through it, somehow still on the road. The highway white and all the fields around them.

Layla handed the beer can back. June had forgotten it. Layla drove on, more slowly than before.

* * *

I don't know what you think of me, Layla said, both eyes on the road, careful. I mean, I know you're a friend and all. But this is just something that I need to do, you know? I know it doesn't make any sense. I know what the practical thing to do is.

You're right, June said. I mean, I know you're right.

I'm just not a practical person, I don't think.

Neither am I, June said. Neither is anybody. We all just pretend to be.

Good luck with that, Layla said.

Oh, for fuck's sake, June said. You treat this like it's an idea, like it's some feeling you're having. Do you even know what's happening to you? I feel like I'm watching a baby walking down the side of a highway, like any minute you're just going to walk out in front of a truck.

Layla didn't say anything, just drove. At the next gravel pullout, she took the truck off the road, put on the emergency brake, stared forward through the windshield.

I didn't know you felt that way, she said.

I'll be better in a minute, June said.

No, Layla said. It's good to know how people feel. Maybe we should go back.

* * *

You don't want to go to the hot springs?

Not today, the girl said. I might hurt my baby. I don't want to hurt *the baby*.

Oh, for fuck's sake, June said.

*

There stands the glass, RL thought as he awoke. All the country songs came true at once: in Mexico with a hangover and a woman who maybe loved him and maybe didn't and blinding light through the long windows. All he lacked was maybe a dog.

She wasn't there, though. Wasn't next to him.

Why not? He searched his memory for the night before, found only scraps and patches, something about an argument, or maybe it was just RL feeling bad. He wondered if he had driven her out. It certainly seemed possible. He didn't feel particularly kind or particularly lovable and he made mistakes, especially when he had been drinking. He felt strangely about her. Maybe he had acted strangely as well.

* * *

A kind of epic pointlessness overtook him, alone in a hotel room far from home and no reason for it.

He went to the window and looked out into the blinding sunlight and there she was: Betsy in her Mayan skirt and sun hat, rounding the corner by the pool. Really, it could have been anyone but it was her, he knew it, if only by the woven bag she carried, a girl who always seemed to be running away from home. What was in there? A bottle of water, of sunblock, of bug spray, a red bandanna and a book about spirituality or vegetarianism. A bedroll. A novel manuscript.

But where was she going? It was only eight o'clock, early on a Sunday morning. Early for the Anglos, anyway. The pool boys in their white shirts and dark skin were well under way, scrubbing down the deep silent blue of the pool. The tables were set, the flowers in their vases. Betsy was the only moving tourist, a flutter of color around the corner of the building and gone. RL knew he had to follow her, though he didn't know why. He scrambled into his tourist clothes, his elaborate sandals and baggy shorts and a fishing hat with a long bill that made him look very stupid. Where was she going? Or: where was she going without him? He hurried down the open staircase, knowing he was already a block or two behind her.

Sleepy Sunday morning, the clanging of the church bells in the village, a mile away. They sounded made of tin. The ocean sat unused and unloved, down past the concrete pool basin, the tile and terraces. He had seen her turn inland and so this was the way he followed, out of the sea breeze, the morning heating up as he walked into the still sunlight. The wind died with the smell of the ocean, and the smell of warm garbage took its place. Across the broad boulevard with its center aisle of palms, he found himself in a mixed, confused neighborhood of battered trucks and rust and animal bones. It looked like a place where work might take place but it was hard to say what kind, some dirty business or drudgery. He followed a red clay lane between two concrete curbs, with more red clay of the same kind on the other side, waiting for something. It looked half done, abandoned in mid-job, this whole place. Ahead, he thought he saw her disappearing into a lane of bright green hedge, a swirl of colorful skirt and gone.

Up close the hedge was glossy-leaved and lethal, long sharp thorns on every branch. He cut his arm on one and the blood dripped down. RL didn't mind the bleeding.

Beyond the fence was another in-between place, half Mexican in its masonry houses and tile roofs but American in its Chevy Suburbans and porch decor. An old man in a white T-shirt and cowboy hat was spraying his gravel yard with Roundup.

Which way? RL started to ask, but the old man just shook his head and pointed with his weed killer bottle to the end of the lane. Went back to his work. This conversation was not to happen. Beyond the next lane of greenery, a community pool of some sort, abandoned. The water sat green and murky a couple of feet below the coping, a permanent stain. Beyond, another gravel walkway, this one lined with brick and spotted with broad, vigorous weeds. The leaves sat low to the ground and matte, dark green, leathery things with spiked white edges. They were alive, they didn't care. Something about these weeds disgusted him. He understood the old man in his hat and poison, the urge to wipe them from the face of the earth. Their insolent vigor.

* * *

At the end of the gravel lane was simply an end; it led to nothing but dead rabbits, cactuses and car parts. He saw her skirt a hundred yards ahead, blue with orange and yellow bands. Morning sun, but he could feel it through the cloth of his hat, unblinking, relentless. Just this far inland and it was like the ocean didn't exist, no sign or scent of it, the red dirt baked into hard piles and things that looked like rabbit castings, dried into lumpy tubes. A half-built house of concrete block. A Monte Carlo up on blocks. RL thought of the oceanside resorts with their white flags flying and their blue water and rustling palms and knew it was unreal, a show put on for the tourists. But this did not feel any more real, skeletal, unfinished . . . like backstage at Disneyland, where he had been once with his high-school band, the dirt and grease and uncollected garbage, cartoon rabbits walking around sweating with their big heads held under their arms . . .

He was almost sure it was her. A blur of bright movement.

The sun flattened all of it into a white picture, desert, sky, spiky thorn plants with red flags of flower at the top. Hard country, alkali white. You could die here. He felt them leave the known world, the last half-empty street, Tecate can, pile of construction debris, forlorn lawn mower. Here was simple, bright and hot. He lost her in and out of the creosote bushes but found her bright skirt again. She never looked back. He never called to her.

RL looked back behind him after a few minutes and saw: nothing, more of the same, open desert and bright sun. He wondered if they were lost.

Betsy kept walking a mile or two.

* * *

You could die here, RL thought, and nobody would know. Maybe they would see the vultures and come looking. Not even ten o'clock in the morning and already all the desert creatures slept down in their holes, in the cool deep dirt or the shade deep under a rock pile. Here where he had no business. No rights in this matter at all.

He realized then that he had not seen her for a few minutes. Betsy had vanished from his sight. RL stopped, and trained his eyes on the spot where he had last seen her, as much as he could tell, but there was nothing. Perhaps he was wrong, a little to the left or to the right. Maybe she had stopped and he hadn't noticed. Maybe RL had caught up to her somehow, or maybe she was even behind him, he had slipped past her, he had turned the wrong way.

When he looked back there was nothing, empty desert and sun.

By the time he had swung his gaze across the whole of the desert, he was lost. Which way was anywhere? A flat mouse-colored hill rose on the horizon but he had not noticed it before, and had no idea whether it was north or south, ocean or inland. He wished sincerely that he had paid a little more attention.

He had nothing with him that might help: no water, no shade, no cell phone.

Burned clean by the sun. This was what she was after, he understood now: the nearness and the dazzle of death, the flat white light. To be lost, let go. He understood water, how it worked and how it went. This place said nothing to him. He stood in his ridiculous clothes, his nylon and polyester, his flaps and buckles, and understood how little it could help him now. Luck would help. Luck and maybe a helping hand. Sunday morning. He stood alone in the amplifying sun and thought: I could do this, I could do that. No way to turn that was better than any other.

His luck was not his to decide. The knowledge of this spilled into him like light, like grace. It was no longer his to do or decide.

This was what she was after, he understood now.

He came upon her kneeling in a clearing of round gray pebbles. Her eyes were closed and her hands pressed together in front of her mouth so that she breathed her own breath. It would hurt to kneel on that ground. She would feel cactus thorns, rocks, goatheads. She would suffer, which, he imagined, was the point. RL stopped moving, said nothing. He felt a kind of golden light coming off her, not just a reflection of the sun but her own light, it was hard to say. It was hard to see her, somehow. He was not worried about his own survival in that moment or hers, either. Something else was going on. He didn't need to understand. As his eyes cleared into the bright dizzying light he saw that behind her praying hands—he was almost sure—Betsy was smiling.

A hot dry wind blew through the creosote branches and ocotillos, making a lonely noise.

She was smiling, he was sure of it. Her eyes were still closed tightly. Not the social smile, the one for others—not the picture-taking smile—but the happiness inside that she couldn't keep off her face. Girl with an ice cream cone. Girl with pet. Girl in love. RL felt an answering joy inside his chest. He could not explain it. He did not try. He felt her like sunlight.

* * *

After a while—later he would try to feel how long, and he wouldn't be able to say—she opened her eyes, but she had known all along that he was there. No surprise. She had been expecting him.

All better now, she said.

*

Hurt, Howard thinks. Drunk and drunk again and not drunk yet.

Lucky Strike casino, eleven o'clock on a Saturday morning, the twenty-seven televisions racketing on about football and Howard thinks of Robert Mitchum in a white T-shirt, smoking an unfiltered cigarette, hurt.

That's what men do, Howard thinks. Take it. You don't have to like it but you do have to take it. Mitchum went to jail for it. The hurting kind. He tried to love her, he did! But she didn't like his style. Wanted to make an asshole out of him. Wanted Howard to play the villain. Well, that was all right, he guessed, a lot of other women out there that God made, a lot of other fish in the sea. Still, she was a fine one. If she only knew what a good man looked like.

She'd be sorry one of these good old days, but Howard would be long gone. He wasn't going to wait around for her to realize.

In the long back hallway, on his way to take a leak, Howard watches the sunlight shine onto the filthy linoleum and thinks of a meadow in May, a meadow with horses and women in it.

Individual particles of dust float through the light. Individual bits of filth on the black floor.

He closes his eyes, standing at the urinal, and thinks of spring sunlight, the horses living in their bodies, running for joy, the arrowleaf balsamroot in yellow flower. Howard himself astride a fast horse, racing for the far green hills. The mountains white above with snow.

When he opens his eyes and looks down, there is blood in the urinal. He closes his eyes again. He doesn't want to see. Another chapter.

American, beautiful, airborne, the Mexicana jet airliner (old, tired, a dent in the side by the passenger door) swoops south into the bluest sky and along the coast and then the long, slow turn out over the ocean, a simple landscape of blue-green water and greenest land cut with red-dirt roads and between land and water a thin white ribbon of sand. . . . It was good, it was beautiful, that thrust and power, that American wallet that solved all the problems. Betsy wants to go home? No problemo, just lay down the wallet, the problems melt and disappear.

He could make out the palms as they curved out over the water but he lost them as they climbed, smaller and gone and only the water below and the fierce tropical sunlight glinting off the bare wings. Speed and power and shine, the pleasant kick back into the seat as the pilot accelerated up into the sky. These Mexican pilots,

RL had to hand it to them: no pause at the end of the runway, no letup in the throttle, just pure noise and thrust. Go and go.

I'm sorry, Betsy said again.

Don't worry about it, RL said again.

When would the drinks cart come? Oh, but here she was already, rattling down the aisle with the seat belt sign barely off and the land still particularized below, the cars and trees and tile-roofed houses like little model railroad sets. . . . If only, RL thought: this feeling of control, of looking at life from high above, the master, the only slightly interested . . . He ordered a gin and tonic, which was free, which made him feel that he would only fly Mexican airlines from here on out.

I knew, Betsy said. All at once I knew.

She was telling her story to herself again. Which was basically fine with RL, he didn't have an argument with her, no hurt feelings though sometimes he did wonder if he had ever been in the room at all or whether it had just been the Betsy and Betsy show all along.

Wings to fly, RL thought. He had checked the Internet in the business center off the hotel lobby and it was twelve degrees at home, the rivers frozen shut, the little birds freezing out of the trees, the deer coming down off the mountain to graze the flower beds. His life made no sense to him. A life of ease and plenty, why not? He had his father's money in the bank, a few million, RL had never touched it but made his own. Dad the bastard, RL thought. His mother weeping in the kitchen. But they were both dead now and unless RL was much, much wrong it would not matter to either of them. RL could spend his father's money on anything he wanted and not betray his mother. The only time he ever touched that money was to keep his mother in assisted living, there at the end, which gave him a feeling of pride mixed with a little bad feeling of revenge. The older he got, the more he missed them. Both of them.

I had to see my kids, Betsy said. I knew it all at once.

Well, that's good, RL said again. I hope you're right.

I am, she said. I just woke up and thought, I am well. Through and through I am well. You believe me.

RL squeezed the last of his lime into his drink, looking down into the icy blue depths of gin. In fact he thought she was crazy. But that didn't mean she was wrong.

You know things I don't, he said.

That's right.

I hope you're right, is all.

She took his hand on the armrest between them and gave it a good squeeze. Her hands were long and fine but years of rough work had made them strong.

You've been good to me, she said. I'll always love you for that. But you have to believe me.

*

Monday morning on her knees again in the incense dark of the church. Her and a bunch of old women. Which June would look like to anybody who even bothered to notice her, another boring story in practical shoes. She would never have her own children. June would never matter. A winter ice-rain spattered against the stained glass.

Layla loved her, she was almost sure. Maybe that was it. Maybe neither one of them could take the heat and press of it, the phantom obligations of love. She couldn't think of Layla now: alone, the thing inside her. Not just the baby but this whole other self, growing out of the wreckage of the old . . . June kept thinking that she would just pick herself up and go on with her life, the way she always had. She was a brave person when she had to be—she had learned that about herself—she could endure. She could suffer. Not a great talent to have. She would rather be able to sing.

And look at her now, sitting in church and thinking about herself. Always herself. Always the bridesmaid.

Jesus floated around her head like some kind of invisible cloud, intangible, just out of reach. June settled herself and pressed her palms together and her lips together and put her shoulders into it, this prayer of hers, but she couldn't touch anything. Nothing solid. Just wishes and hopes, stories and pictures, the sacred bleeding heart and the Virgin assumed whole and torpedo-shaped into Heaven. And June, the non-virgin non-birth. *Barren*, is what the Bible would call her, barren among women. The fruit of thy womb.

This was getting her nowhere.

She didn't have to work until the next day. No particular place to go.

But this was still getting her nowhere, the dark that wouldn't answer, the great uncommunicative cloud of Jesus. . . . June was restless, restless. She felt like she needed to find some orphan somewhere, something, anything that needed taken care of. Some flightless baby bird. She zipped herself into her fleece jacket. This is June at forty-nine: a Polarfleece beret, a fuzzy brick-colored polyester jacket with fake Mayan trim, wool stockings and brown comfortable shoes. Everything fits into her little bag: her cell phone, wallet, the various medications she must take. She fits together like a jigsaw puzzle. A couple of pieces missing.

* * *

Outside, gray and nowhere. She wished just once that she could hear Taylor play his trombone again.

She's staying at the downtown Holiday Inn for now, until she can find a place. Her things are scattered where she left them, at Howard's, at the ministorage, in RL's garage. She has an appointment with a financial adviser at three o'clock to talk about what to do with all her money. As of today, she has three million two hundred and thirty thousand dollars in her checking account, which seems not quite right. Maybe she should buy a car or two. A nice little neighborhood to call her own. She doesn't cry, June doesn't, but if she did, this would be the morning for it.

Maybe she will take herself to lunch.

There's nothing for her on this side of the river, anyway, and so she starts back downtown again, hopscotching through the alleys in the half rain. These neighborhoods were old and still mostly cheap, polite from the front—all chain-link lawns and tidy mailboxes— but the back alleys were full of personality, canoes and derelict Bonnevilles, woodpiles, curious malamutes, men smoking in their underwear. The rain filled the puddles, sparkled on the lawn mowers and windows. Last year's gardens sat abandoned and brown in tidy rows, waiting for planting, and somewhere here (maybe in the next block) was an amazing wishing well of concrete with bits of shattered dinner plates set in to decorate, a rooster painted on one of them that had been part of her grandmother's china set, a little bit of her set in concrete forever, or till the weather faded it to nothing. . . .

A little dog looked back at her from the block ahead. Not that little but long and low. Not a wiener dog exactly but furry, alert. It stood sideways across the alley and pointed its big radar ears at her, mouth a little open, eyes bright.

Then he turned, and walked off.

This was Dorris MacKintyre's house, was it not? June was almost sure of it. She had been here several times but never from the alley, never from this angle. The curtain closed in the window. A little shiver down her neck: this was perhaps not good news. She stood up next to the house and looked up, the way she would if she were looking out the window, and there were Dorris's squirrels chattering and racing along the wires. Oh, hello, she thought, hello, good-bye.

That little dog again, from the next block. It looked like he was laughing at her. Dirty fur, small feet, nimble, gone.

Oh, Dorris, she thought. A good death. June prayed he wasn't lingering behind closed curtains, the way they held on sometimes. June wanted the best for the people she loved, and she loved them all. Maybe that was the problem. Maybe her heart was just taken, maybe Taylor had stolen it away with him, and all that was left was this general love, this nice feeling. She thought of Layla, then, of Layla's idiocies and passions, her confusions and trouble, and for that moment June was passionately jealous. She wanted only what Layla had, the ability to give herself, forget herself, to die, to burn. To die for love.

It was a nice thought.

It wasn't her.

* * *

That little dog was up beside her then, and looking at her. He didn't have a collar, June supposed it was a he, something about a general look. He was three colors: black, white and a really lovely honey-brown mixed in. He had white delicate feet, soiled with spring mud, and a nice little white blaze on the back of his neck. He watched her expectantly from three feet away.

Well, hello, she said.

The dog didn't move, just grinned and watched.

Whose little dog are you? June asked.

The dog looked into her eyes insistently but without aggression or need. June felt that he was trying to tell her something. She started to walk again but he just walked with her. When she stopped, he stopped. When she started again, he walked with her.

Who are you? she asked again, but the dog just looked at her.

She walked to the end of the alley and turned onto the sidewalk, and the little dog followed easily at her heel. Apparently she had a dog now. Apparently she was a dog owner. Last fall's leaves were plastered in decaying relief on the wet sidewalk and a girl was crying, halfway up the block. Not a little girl, either, but a high school girl or so with tattoos and black hair. June knew this girl. Who was she?

Greta, she said.

The girl looked up at her, surprised. Raccoon rings of eye shadow dripped down her cheeks in the tears and rain. June raced toward her, handkerchief at the ready, her little dog by her side.

* * *

You're a mess, she said, swiping vigorously at the girl's face. What's the matter?

W—w—w—w, said the girl.

Don't talk, June said. She gathered the girl into her arms, there on the sidewalk, felt her try to wrestle away—like a wild thing, the natural resistance—then relax into her embrace. Through the ver-tebrae of the girl's back, June felt the convulsions inside, quiet involuntary sobbing that didn't quite make it out into the air. June held on for dear life. Who was getting what out of this? Who was this *for*, exactly? But it didn't matter: it was a good thing, touch, and a good thing was good, whatever the reason. Round and round. She looked at the little dog over the girl's shoulder and his brown eyes seemed deep and sympathetic.

What is it? June whispered. What's the matter?

B—b—b—b, said the girl.

What?

Bitch, the girl said. Leave me alone, bitch.

She tore her body from June's and balled up into herself again, but June would not leave her alone. June put her hand around the girl's shoulders.

Leave me alone, the girl said.

Is it your grandfather?

* * *

Greta looked up at her, slapped.

How do you know about my grandfather?

I take care of him sometimes, June said. I'm with the hospice.

Oh, that's you.

Yeah.

No, it's not him. It's not that.

What?

We're getting kicked out, Greta said. A kind of pride in the way she said it, a kind of deliberate offense. She said, They closed the 4B's and my mom lost her job.

What are you going to do?

I don't know.

Where are you going to go?

Greta just looked at her like the question itself was an insult, which maybe it was. June saw herself through the girl's eyes, rich bitch looking down at her. People worked in this life. People didn't just get lucky. Though June had an argument with her luck. A bone to pick.

It's just money? June asked.

* * *

Greta shrugged.

Well, that's easy, June said. I've got money.

Greta looked at her like she was being tricked and June felt all naked all of a sudden. It was the right thing to do—God knows she had money—but the wrong thing just the way she had the power now, and all this little girl had was trouble. Looking down at her. June needed comfort, assurance, and she reached down to pet the little dog on its belly, the little dog that followed her.

Look out, Greta said.

But it was too late. The dog had already bitten her hand, a sudden unexpected snarling frenzy, and then retreated to the parking strip, where it stood looking at her, hackles up, expecting to be beaten.

They had a kid, a boy, Greta said. There was something wrong with him. He used to go after that dog with a broom handle.

June looked down to see if her hand was bleeding and it was but only a little bit.

Who did?

What?

Who had the boy, the dog, the broom handle?

The Freys, Greta said. They used to live down on the corner. They were bastard people.

* * *

They just moved away, June said.

And left the dog, Greta said. We feed him. So does everybody else.

What's her name?

His.

What's his name, then?

Spode, Greta said.

Spode, June said. She looked over to the dog where he was waiting to be beaten. He was not a perfect dog. He was somebody else's problem. She looked down at her hand where he had bitten her and knew that Spode would bite other people. There would be arguments, threats, ugly surprises about the nature of the people she knew. She might lose an acquaintance or two over this dog, she thought.

Come here, boy, she said.

*

Well, RL said.

Don't say it. Don't say a word.

OK.

Just for a moment.

In the mud and snow at the foot of her road, the skeleton trees
and alders. In a little clearing. Trucks racing by invisible on Highway 35, a few feet away, a road-killed deer frozen in the borrow pit.
RL got out to turn the hubs, to make the mudslide road up to her
place. When he was done with the passenger side, he stood up and
there she was. Then they were kissing.

* * *

Seems like a dream, she said, and RL said, Mexico.

So far away.

You're sure you want to . . .

Betsy laughed. Poor Robert, she said. Whatever you wanted, I'm sure it wasn't this.

I'm all right, he said.

I know.

This was just what I had in mind, he said. All along.

It found me, Betsy said. I couldn't have done it without you. It found me and it will find you.

What did?

Grace, she said. I once was lost but now I'm found.

This sudden fervent frantic need to believe, down deep inside him. She was right, she had to be right, to be healed. RL felt like there was something there, something he couldn't name, standing beside him. RL felt *light*.

It will find you, Betsy said.

*

Having tried, having failed, having loved, having fucked it up, RL turns toward home. Toward *house*, he corrects himself; then relents. As long as Layla's there, it's home. After that, February.

We'll be drinking early today.

He's made a fool of himself. Everybody knows, June and Layla, put it in the paper! They'd all been right and he'd been wrong. A very public fool. His luggage from Mexico sits still behind the seat and for a moment he'll just go back to the airport, catch the next flight for anywhere. Right back in the fallen world, he thinks. Everything stale and dull and usual is waiting for him. She was his ticket out, his escape. Now she's made her getaway without him.

* * *

A feeling inside that he just wants to vomit out. No direction, no next step.

RL curses out loud, beats the steering wheel with the palm of his hand.

RL thinks about turning back, back up the long road to her house. But you can't rescue a person from herself. She does not wish to be rescued. She wants to be left alone with her children and the awful Roy. RL doesn't understand but his lack of understanding will not change a thing. He is alone in the world again.

Alone: and without a plan.

RL doesn't know what he wants, except that he wants a drink. And here is the Clearwater Bar! What luck!

Outside the sky is pearly gray and darkening toward night, a promise of snow in the fat air. RL is still fifty miles of bad curvy road from home. Just one, he thinks. A thought he has had before, he knows it. Maybe he should get a dog. A reason to live. Layla, he reminds himself: reason enough. Too many cars in the parking lot for this time of a Tuesday afternoon, and tinkly music leaking out of the door frame gives RL a bad premonition.

Chicken and dumplings? says the man on the stool by the door.

I was just going to get a drink, RL says.

Go ahead and suit yourself, says the door man, an elderly gent with bright white false teeth. I'm just saying, it's chicken and dumplings night. You get hungry, come on back here and pay up. Five bucks! All you can eat!

Will do, says RL. His bad dream is coming true in waves, a bar full of old men and old women, all of them in the old-style Western polyester, the kind that just doesn't wear out, pearl snaps on the men and embroidery, even occasional fringe on the ladies. RL is the youngest person here by an easy ten years. Everybody smoking, everybody drinking whiskey ditches, rye and ginger, Merle Haggard and the Strangers on the jukebox singing, swinging doors, a jukebox and a barstool . . . and all of them with plates on the table of steaming chicken, golden gravy, fat white dumplings and green peas. RL waited his turn at the bar—busy night, the bartender running her shoes off—and remembered the cafeteria in his junior high school, that same food smell, though here mixed with the spilled beer, Lysol and cigarette reek of a working bar.

He feels the night enfolding him like some fever dream, unreal and evil, the laughing faces and the blur of bar noise. In silence, but with a knowing look, the bartender brings him a Daniel's on the rocks and takes his money and brings him change but when she hands him the silver, she looks at him significantly, as if some other currency was being exchanged. . . . Her hands, anyway, are long and slender with pointed delicate nails, beautiful except for the red welted scar that runs across the back of her left hand. The wood of the bar is grooved deeply where old men have rubbed their quarters into it, year after year, making deep ruts and scars in the old wood, polished smooth by the loving fingers of the old men, daytime drinkers, time-wasters. RL knows it's only the damage, only the hours and miles since Mexico— was that only this morning? it was, it was—but something is settling into him, seeping in, some kind of subtle poison.

* * *

Then two couples start to dance, except it's not exactly dancing, what they're doing, all the moves of a dance but no grace, no smoothness, no fluidity of movement, like a series of freeze-frames all spliced together and an expression of great seriousness, almost of suffering, on the faces of the men. Chicken and dumplings, RL thinks, chicken and dumplings. The women with their plump cheeks like dumplings, white. They smile up at their stone-faced partners but the smile is just on the surface of their faces, just a mask for something deeper, something inside RL, too, the certainty of loss. Like a bell ringing a bell, this suffering sent from one mind to the answering silence. She's gone. She's not coming back. He is alone. *Alone*, echoes the face of the ranch wife in her Western dress, circling the dance floor like a tired boxer. *Alone*, say the hands of the bartender, the smell of chicken and dumplings, the smoke that sits in settled layers in the hot air of the bar.

RL drains his drink, and heads for the exit.

You'll be back! says the door man. Nobody comes to chicken and dumplings just once. Everybody comes back.

The feeling of dream does not leave him even out in the parking lot, even on the highway again. Lights on, the darkening afternoon, he feels like he could just reach out and put his hand through it, insubstantial as wet paper. In a minute it starts to snow, and the individual white flakes stream and swim through his headlights. Here he is, again inside the whirlwind. Here he is again, and gone.

*

I couldn't have him at the motel, June said.

No, Layla said. Come on in.

I missed you anyway.

Oh, crap.

What?

Me, too.

The snow sifting down onto the wet street behind her, a few flakes melting into her hair.

Pissing on a round flat rock as the snow falls all around him through the black trees and the Blackfoot tumbles over a shallow riffle twenty feet away. Where did Christmas go? Alone in the forest.

*

Alone in his studio, a little room carved out of one end of the garage—but his own, all his—Edgar sees that the real winter has begun, gray pearly skies and white snow. Bring it on, he thinks. Let it snow up to the eaves, let the river freeze solid. Wipe the whole town out in a smear of pure white. Let it *erase.*

He thinks about turning the radio on, decides not to. Thinks about going up to the house to make himself a cup of tea, which would be nice. But Amy and the girl are napping, at least they were a few minutes ago, and he doesn't want to wake them. Four o'clock. There's a little dorm fridge in the corner with a couple of bottles of beer in it, good beer. Four o'clock is a little early. But not *really* early. And besides, it's snowing, a holiday feel, a time out of regular life. A swirly, damp snow, fat flakes drifting down, a snow-globe snow . . .

* * *

A beer then. He opens it and regards the work on his drawing table, a pencil sketch of her face. He hasn't seen her in a month but he can't seem to stop himself. It's a little obsessive, he knows it—poking the sore place, the absence, over and over again until it burns—but it's also become a kind of meditation. Always the same face but never the same face twice. Like weather, the little currents of feeling that play over her features, a little happy, a little annoyed, the infinite fine gradations of feeling and all mixed together. This one, maybe, is a memory of the ferry ride to the island: happy and excited, the sea breeze stirring up her blood, but a little fearful, doubtful. . . . It was just easier to draw than to put into words, because the words made everything separate, like they were different things, but on her face they were just one complicated feeling all together. The face: where the inner person, the stranger, unknowable, surfaced a little into the world. It was all there, you just had to know how to look.

Maybe if he stands across the street, he might see her through the window.

Maybe she's back in Seattle already.

Between the cell phone, the text message, the Internet and instant messaging, it's almost harder to stay out of touch than it is to keep in contact. It requires an act of the will. Edgar's will works only intermittently. She has already disappeared from Facebook. The last contact, a text message he sent her at three in the morning, *Where are you?* and her wan reply, *I'm here.*

He understands that he needs to see her.

* * *

He understands that he has no excuse. He's just going. Some-where. Out. The other side of the door. He'll find a way to explain to Amy later, or he won't.

Fortunately he's wearing waterproof hiking boots already, his winter uniform, has his wool coat at the ready and his stocking cap. He leaves the beer on the bookcase by the door and starts off into the milky afternoon, the quiet, settled snow. He turns back, when he reaches the alley, and sees that the snow has almost erased his footprints. Erase, he thinks. Make it new again. Make it clean.

*

And so, when RL finally gets back home, the last hard slog from Bonner through town, a dozen accidents on the snow-slick freeway and the flashing lights through the pelting snow—emergency, emergency—and then the crawl across the university district with insane hippie bicyclists invisible in the snow and up the long hill, he is expecting nothing, instead finds every window lit, a strange Prius in the driveway, or is it June's? And who is that other head in the living room window?

All in dreams he takes his suitcase from behind the seat where it had warmed by the heater and smells the coconut aroma of sunblock. All in a day. The world seems a small and senseless place and RL has no place in it. But at least he is home, home at last.

* * *

The conversation just drops off the table when he walks through the door. And what the hell. Edgar.

June says, Welcome home, hello.

Layla says, How was Mexico?

Edgar doesn't say anything at all.

RL looks from face to face in a dream. All in a circle without him.

What is it? RL asks. What's happening?

They look from face to face, all at one another and none of them at him. Finally June turns to him.

You look exhausted, she says.

Please, RL says. Is someone dead? Who's dead?

No one has died, June says. Nothing terrible has happened.

Please, RL says, and looks at Edgar, his employee, for Christ sake, he has to tell him, takes a step to take Edgar by the shirtfront and shake the fact out of him, whatever it is.

No one is in the hospital, June says.

Layla says, Sit down. Sit down before you fall down.

I'm all right.

* * *

You look like your own ghost, his daughter says. Sit down.

He doesn't want to. But he does anyway, takes a place at the kitchen table. June takes a place there, too, and Layla brings him a glass of water, and then sits, too. Edgar says, I really have to go.

No, Layla says. Stay.

Edgar looks fearfully from her face to RL's and back but he obeys. Takes a place at the table. Like poker, RL thinks, the four of them sitting around. Like Indian poker, he thinks, where everybody but you knows what you've got.

I'm going to have a baby, Layla says. That's all.

The news hits him in his body, his belly, the same place Betsy hurt him. He has failed. The others are all looking at him and RL feels naked in their gaze, helpless. This was why he is here, the whole point of him is to take care of her, to protect her. In this he had failed. In all their eyes.

Now the women were taking care of him. They looked at him with kindness and concern. More than he could bear.

Then looked at Edgar, and understood why he was present. Edgar wouldn't meet his eye.

The two of you, he said, aiming his head at Layla, Edgar, back to Layla.

For a while now, Layla said.

* * *

All this brisk feminine truth-telling. RL didn't want any more of it. He longed for his illusions—that he was happy, that he was loved, that he was taking care of his people, that he even knew his people. He looked from face to face and knew that it was a lie. A lie that he loved. A series of lies.

And you, he thinks, turning to Edgar, who still won't meet his eye: What about you, Edgar?

What have you got to say for yourself? RL asks him.

Not much.

What does your wife think?

That got a rise out of him. RL sees this with some small satisfaction.

Amy doesn't know. I don't think she knows.

Are you going to tell her?

I don't know what I'm going to do, Robert. I really don't. I'm going to go, I think.

He turns to June, who is clearly running the show. He asks, Is that all right? I was supposed to be home a while ago.

No, go.

RL watches him seek out Layla's eyes but she won't give them to him. He has hurt her, RL sees. Hurt his daughter.

*

Go, Layla tries to tell him. Go now. She tries to stare him out the door, but something fatal lingers. Edgar! Her poor little heart is full of fear and pounding. Go!

This awful calm. Nothing is happening. Everything is about to.

I love you, she thinks. Then whispers it, not quite aloud, the way she used to say her prayers: I love you.

*

And June the restraining hand on his forearm and
he notices, she's touching him, and for a moment it might work, he
might stop but he doesn't stop.

*

And Edgar, out in the flurrying swirling snow full dark and fat individual flakes in the porch light, he is out and alone with a feeling of escape. Not just from RL but from the women, too, and from the impossibility. From himself, perhaps. A last backward glance before he steps into a run, toward home, that momentary hesitation . . .

And just then the door opens outward and RL through it in a rhino charge that carries him to Edgar in one motion and then both of them down and scrambling in the wet snow. Someone is hitting Edgar in the stomach. A taste of blood in his mouth and his mind a blank all confusion and the women watching from the porch and Edgar wants no part of this. He stands—he tries to stand—the snow slips from under his feet and RL hits him in the face. Blood and snot spatter across the white snow and enough, Edgar thinks, is enough.

* * *

RL is standing back to admire the effect of his punch, blood in the porch light, blood on the snow, when Edgar stands him up with a short chop punch to the Adam's apple and then six punches to his big soft gut. RL goes down like a bag of shit. Edgar kicks him in the side of his head and he goes out. This last is extra. Edgar never meant to but his blood is up, he's blind with it.

Layla cries out at the kick, animal, something short and sharp torn from her.

That's enough, says June.

Then it's over. Blood courses down the front of his shirt and RL lies still in the snow. Edgar stands there breathing. June comes and kneels next to RL in the snow.

Is he . . . says Edgar.

Get out of here, says Layla. Just go.

Sill he hesitates.

I'll call the cops, Layla says. I will.

He looks at her but he's just dead. He turns to go, turns back to see, but there is nothing here for him, no warmth, no light, no curiosity. Some things you don't recover from, he thinks. Some things just end. He starts into the darkness, starts to run, because it's too cold to walk, the blood still up in him, his face wet with it. The taste of blood in his mouth. This end of things, he thinks. Faster.

*

After: RL lying in his big empty bed. He must have slept for a little while but now he's wide awake. It's dark outside the windows, a little light coming through under the closed door. The wind whistles in the eaves of the house. Sometimes he hears the women moving quietly on the floor below, trying not to bother him, not to wake him. Their low voices, soft movements.

Funereal, he thinks.

This end of things.

And where from here? He saw it in his daughter's face, in June's face: they were done with him. Disgusted. He wasn't particularly fond of himself, either, not just at this moment. His windpipe was hot and sore, his gut. A big black eye. A white-light headache. No more than he deserved, RL supposed. What next? But there was only endurance, a blank place, a series of days to get through.

Layla and her baby. What to even feel.

A hope and a light that fades quickly to nothing. She won't keep it, she couldn't. In the end it will just be another injury, a bad experience, keep it in a box to keep the smell down. The last years of his marriage to Dawn. Maybe Betsy, soon enough. The things that started out in love and light and hope and then became just nothing, or worse than nothing. He's acted badly with Dawn, badly with Edgar. Ashes, rust, a taste of pennies in his mouth. Railroad dirt that smells like petroleum. Inside he feels like the edge of town that trails off into tank farms and trailer parks and switching yards, a wilderness of cold steel. Bits of broken glass shining in the gravel and low-hanging power lines overhead, not even hell but just abandoned, uncared for. What he's made of himself. Nobody made this but himself. This would not kill him, he knew that, he was too stubborn and stupid for suicide and he wouldn't drink himself to death, he was almost sure. He hadn't at the end of things with Dawn. But he had Layla then, Layla to take care of, the love of a child to see him through. What would sustain him now?

RL is being dramatic. He still has Layla to look after.

Not the same, though, not the daily business of school and breakfast. She's making her own mistakes now. And RL's job is to let go, not to hold on. And she has seen him weak, and seen him stupid, and violent. He feels his face flush in the dark, though there is no one to be embarrassed in front of. He's alone now, in a dark room, awake and burning with shame. Alone.

* * *

Alone; or so it seems.

It takes him a minute to realize that the door is open an inch, a crack of light dim but real in the dark bedroom, one of the women standing there, watching him. Which one? and how long? He thought for a moment that he might have been asleep, but no. Just tied up in his own self-pity and misery.

He raises himself on one elbow to see who it is.

June enters the bedroom, shuts the door behind her with a solid quiet click, comes to his bed and lies down next to him, not touching. The far side of the bed, and it's a big bed, a California king. Each of them lies on their back, pillow under their head, eyes toward the ceiling, breathing.

I have certainly made a mess of things, June says.

RL considers this and says, Not more than me.

No, June says. Not more than you. But a mess anyway. All this money and nowhere to go.

RL stares at the dark ceiling, each of them alone, adrift. Nap time, he thinks, remembering afternoons in the dim recesses of his own childhood, the sound of blue jeans turning in the dryer downstairs, the smell of ironing.

You can stay here, he finally says. As long as you want to.

Thank you.

* * *

No, I mean it, RL says. Layla loves you. And God knows I could use the help.

I've been thinking about it, June says; and something in her voice surprises him, some new emotion or sound, he can't put his finger on it.

She says, This has to stop, you know? I've been thinking about it. It's just too much sadness, too much confusion. You can't put one day on top of the next to save your life. And I'm no better. I'm used to thinking of myself as better off, but I'm not. Just this whirlwind. It has to stop.

The whirlwind, RL thinks. *Stuck in the motherfucking vortex.*

He says, I know. But what can we do?

I've been thinking about this, June says. Then, to his great surprise, she laces her own small cold hand into his.

RL begins to weep. She doesn't see.

We take care of each other, she says. We try.

RL holds onto her hand as he waits until his weakness passes and it is safe to talk again. A minute that stretches into three or four. Chicken and dumplings, says a voice in his head. Chicken and dumplings, chicken and dumplings, chicken and dumplings. Around and around and finally it slowly fades.

Can you just do that? he asks. Can you just try and then make something happen?

* * *

That I do not know, June says.

I can't do worse, he says.

We've tried not trying, she said. We've tried to live with whatever chance brought us. That is how we got here.

Well, RL said. I guess we'll find out.

I guess we will.

She gives his hand a little understated squeeze and RL finds this thrilling. More than he expected. So much more than he had any right to expect, He feels a tear gather in his chest.

Then the door bursts open and Layla comes in, not seeing them in the dark, not expecting them, their hands fly apart like independent wings as her eyes adjust to the dark and sees them there on the big bed.

I wondered where you two had gotten to, she says.

RL tries to think of what he might say but he doesn't need to. His daughter closes the door most of the way, a sliver of dim light to illuminate the three of them, then lies down herself between them on the bed with her head down at the foot end. Just flops down flat.

After a minute she says, I have made such a mess of things.

And Layla is surprised when both June and her father start to laugh, loud genuine laughter.

* * *

What? she says. What's so funny?

But in this moment neither one of them can stop to tell her, the laughter feeds on itself unwholesome like the laughter at a funeral or accident but still contagious and after a minute of this, of giggle and calm and then the laughter bursting forth again, Layla herself joins in, against her own heart, against her own sorrow but she laughs and June and RL laughs and Spode, the little dog, Spode hears them and noses the bedroom door open and sees the three of them together on the bed and knows in his dog heart this is where he should be as well. He is not going to be left out again. From the doorway at full stride he runs and when he reaches the bed he leaps and none of them are expecting this furball missile all teeth and play and this sets them off again and it will be a while, now, before the laughter stops.

*

Spring, he saw it first on the hillside above town in the shape of a glacier lily, a yellow bell of a flower, small and shy among the weeds. Edgar stopped running to look at it but when he stopped the wind cut through him. Through his nylon jacket he could feel approaching snow. Black clouds, rain or snow out over Lolo.

But still, spring.

He ran full tilt down Cherry Gulch, past the dog walkers and bird-watchers, scaring up a flock of bluebirds as he ran, little bursts of pure bright color in the corners of his sight, a few robins, too, and the ever-present crows. The steeps of the trail hurt his knees to run but he wanted that, a little. Slipping and sliding on the gravel, counting on gravity to see him through, he passed the same gray-braided birder that he did nearly every week, a last spring maybe.

She looked like she knew something, like she had something to tell him, but she just smiled at him in a knowing way as he hurried past. Her binoculars and walking sticks. To be old, to be graceful, to be alert and interested. To be out in the weather, any weather, with her parka tied around her waist.

He hadn't been to the new house, but he knew where it was from looking it up on the Internet. He had seen it from space, the green metal shingles of the roof.

When he wasn't feeling sorry for himself, Edgar thought this was a wonderful world, with beautiful people in it, and occasional miracles.

What a fancy street this was, though. Right down next to the creek. All redwood and privacy fences, big Toyota SUVs in the driveways, little Minis, fun cars, cars for fun. Pretty women gardening in gardening clothes. Edgar wasn't used to thinking about this as a town where people had money—they kept to themselves, the people with money, and didn't show it much. Up in their log châteaus by the ski area or here, with a pretty little creek running through the backyard and nice quiet neighbors. People like us, Edgar thought. People with easy lives.

Now RL had joined up with them. Edgar didn't work at the fly shop anymore and so it was technically none of his business but still, a disappointment. Where had the money come from?

The house itself was nice enough: pleasant, reasonable. It was mostly red-brown wood on the outside and not too fancy, with a couple of solar panels up on the roof and trees all around. The place next door was huge and white with plantation pillars all around the porch but apart from that, RL's house seemed like a reasonable place, a place where a person might be happy. A girl. He hadn't seen her in three months.

Where a girl like her might be happy without him.

He hadn't seen her since that night. Now he stood at the end of the walkway considering. He didn't know what to hope for. He didn't want anything from her. He didn't even want to bother her and he knew that his presence would, it would bother her. He should really just go, back to the river and across, back to the house on the south side. He should forget her, as she had forgotten him.

But there was something real there, some betrayal. This was happiness itself. They made each other happy, when they weren't making each other miserable, which was most of the time. Still it was real and he couldn't just walk away. Run away.

He couldn't move, either. Stuck to the street like a piece of spent gum.

His feet carried him toward the door, unwilling and wanting and unsure. This new house where she lived. RL might be there, which Edgar was afraid of, though he believed RL to know nothing of this. This was dangerous and stupid. Edgar himself: dangerous and stupid.

The door opened before he could reach it and the little dog battered and barked against the screen.

Spode, the woman said. Spode! Cut it out.

* * *

I was looking for Layla, Edgar said.

She's not here.

Is there another time? I could . . .

No, June said. She opened the screen and the little dog rushed out at him, not such a little dog, really, but alert and sharp. Bright little eyes. He wanted to jump up on Edgar's leg but kept himself from doing so by exercising some restraint.

June's face was kind. She said, She's not here, Edgar.

Is she in town?

No, June said. No she's not.

Is there any way that I can get in touch with her?

I don't think so, June said. She needed to get away for a while. It was a hard winter for her.

No, Edgar said, I know.

But he didn't know anything—he saw it in her face, that almost contempt. She knew, he didn't. She knew he didn't. He felt himself shrinking—but she didn't mean to be unkind. She reached her hand out and touched him on the arm.

I'll let her know you came looking for her, June said.

Thank you, Edgar said. Is RL . . .

* * *

He's down in Costa Rica, June said, building houses for poor people. Habitat for Humanity. I know! It's not like him at all, is it?

I don't know, Edgar said.

I think he surprised himself with that one, June said. Oh, well, come on, Spode. Come on back in.

The little dog—a handsome little dog, a little smarty-pants—took one last searching look at Edgar to make sure that he didn't need to defend the house against him. Then he turned and went through the open screen, and June gave him a little shrug, let the screen close, closed the door behind it. There was nothing left to do but turn and go. He walked to the street, the cold wind blowing up out of the south. He would be lucky to get home without being rained on, or even snow. At the street he turned for one last look before he started to run again, a look back toward the house with its framing trees and solar panels and there, up on the roof—he hadn't noticed it before—at the peak of the house was a fieldstone chimney, and as he watched a single puff of white smoke came out. Just that, a single breath and nothing more. He turned, then, and started to run again. But all the way home he wondered about it, saw it in his mind: a ragged cloud of white against the dark spring sky, a bit of vapor, of nothing, and yet he recognized it: the start of something.

Kevin Canty is the award-winning author of the novels *Into the Great Wide Open*, *Nine Below Zero* and *Winslow in Love*, as well as the short story collections *Honeymoon and Other Stories*, *A Stranger in This World* and *Where the Money Went*. His work has been published in *The New Yorker*, *Esquire*, *GQ*, *Details*, *Story*, *New York Times Magazine* and *Glimmer Train*. He currently teaches fiction writing at the University of Montana.

This book was set in Janson, a typeface long thought to have been made by the Dutchman Anton Janson, who was a practicing typefounder in Leipzig during the years 1668–1687. However, it has been conclusively demonstrated that these types are actually the work of Nicholas Kis (1650–1702), a Hungarian, who most probably learned his trade from the master Dutch typefounder Dirk Voskens. The type is an excellent example of the influential and sturdy Dutch types that prevailed in England up to the time William Caslon (1692–1766) developed his own incomparable designs from them.

1